RESCUED BY THE SURLY WOODSMAN

HALEY TRAVIS

1

SAGE

Um... Have I walked into a cartoon?

He doesn't look real. Blinking hard, I shake my head and look again.

Nope, he's real.

I break into a spontaneous smile as the little guy hops to another branch. It's a fairly common blue-winged warbler, but he has unusually bright coloring. His head and body are a warm sunny yellow, with stunning bright blue wings. There's a sweet little white patch on his shoulder that's a perfect triangle.

Taking a few photos, I stay perfectly silent. Then he flits two trees farther away. My feet move slowly down the path, my breathing quiet and calm. Each motion is as smooth as possible. A breeze whispers through the top branches of the trees, yet everything else is still.

Every time I get closer, I snap only a few pics before he jumps somewhere else. I wish I could explain that if he would take just a moment out of his morning to stay still, I could make some money from his portrait. But I doubt that adorable birds with cool markings understand stock photographs or nature blogs.

There are other birds around, yet I keep my camera squarely trained on Hoppy, meandering slightly to the west.

The ground around here is damp and covered in leaves and sticks, but looks perfectly safe. I make a marker of three fallen sticks, lining them up in a tidy row before stepping off the mountain trail. Several hundred feet later, I make another one.

I've heard stories of people getting lost in the forest, so leaving myself signposts like these is crucial. I'm really not that far from the trail, but still I take a mental note of how far I've come, especially when I walk around a bit of a ridge and past some massive boulders.

Hoppy jumps down to a lower branch, and somehow – Oh! – bounces right into a beam of sunlight dancing through the forest.

Snap.

I take as many shots as I can as fast as I can, but I think that first one was the winner.

Although I don't want to push my luck, I can't help but creep closer as he darts to another tree and into a nook on a fluffy pine branch where the white triangle on his shoulder is right in another patch of light. Then the light dims, as a huge incoming cloud bank moves over the mountain.

I line up my shot, zooming in as much as I can without distortion, then slowly walk closer.

I scream as my foot slides out from under me and sideways into a jagged branch. The wood pierces right through my sneaker and into my skin, while I land on my butt, hard.

The warbler looks down at me, blinks, then flies away at top speed.

Ow ow freakin' OW.

At least my camera landed on my stomach instead of on the ground. I take a moment to catch my breath, my foot already throbbing with a sickening, stabbing pain. My butt and hip begin to ache from landing with my full weight on my hip bone.

The sun dips over the mountain, and the forest darkens as if someone had turned down a dimmer switch.

I check my phone. *Crap.* I thought I had another twenty minutes of daylight before dark.

And I haven't heard anyone else out here on the trails over the past hour or so.

Tears prick my eyes as I consider my rotten luck. Why couldn't this have happened this morning, when there were a ton of hikers around? I mean, sure, they scared off a lot of the birds, but at least I wouldn't be out here completely alone.

I pack away my camera safely, then take a deep breath and try to stand. *Owww.* Seriously bad idea. Putting any weight on that foot makes the open wound rub against the torn canvas. Plus, it's so slippery right here that I might fall on my face next time.

"Hello?" I holler in the direction of the trail.

No answer. There is a huge boulder directly between me and the trail, and I can't exactly shout straight through it. As well, there are so many trees that they muffle the sound, making it almost impossible to project in a single direction. Still, I'll have to try.

I scream my head off for five minutes straight until my voice gives out and I start to sound like an old blues singer. Once I'm forced to give up...my throat is starting to ache as much as my foot...I assess the situation.

Mental pep talk time. *All you have to do is rest for a minute, then find a way to stand up.* Maybe I can use a sturdy tree as a crutch, and hobble to the trail. Yeah. That'll work.

Then thunder rumbles in the distance, sending a shiver up my spine.

So much for returning to the charming small town of Old Hemlock Valley tonight for some food before finding a safe place to park the car and sleeping in the back seat. Now the goal is to make it back to the parking lot at the trailhead and use my car for shelter.

Was that a voice calling out? It was too faint to be sure. I call back, but my voice is blown out. Gathering up my things, I try to roll to the side, then bring myself to kneeling.

Some twigs snap right beside the boulder. I shrink back in shock.

Oh my... Is that a bear?

No. A gigantic man is lumbering toward me!

He's definitely a local mountain guy, wearing a green plaid flannel shirt, well worn jeans, and work boots. And his thick arms have definitely chopped down a few trees.

He's tall, dark and, frankly, grouchy looking, but there's something about him that radiates strength and confidence. He's obviously the kind of take-charge guy who will probably think I'm a pitiful mess.

As he comes closer, my mouth falls open in shock at the warmth and depth in his beautiful dark hazel eyes.

It doesn't matter that he's scowling as if I've just ruined his day.

He's gorgeous. No, not just gorgeous... He's panty-drenching *sexy*.

2

BARRETT

roceries? *Check.*

Gas? *Check.*

Library? *Check.*

Dealing with way more people than I want to in a single day? *Triple flipping check.*

The people in Old Hemlock Valley are decent, honest, hard-working folks. Even better, they leave me alone.

I'm polite enough, of course. Especially to little old Mrs. Fergus at the library, who always puts "those crazy spy thrillers you love so much, dear" on hold for me when something new comes in. Yet even with that sweet lady, who might as well be the entire town's grandma, a few minutes of book chat is plenty.

I stow my bags in the back of my pickup, then jump in to head home. A few miles down the road, I slow down at the turnoff. Should I...? Half an hour till sundown. Yeah, I should.

I reluctantly turn off the main road to check the trailhead just a quarter mile down. Hopefully I'll see a familiar truck or two, and know that Jace or Baz are taking a look. Rolling into the gravel parking area... No such luck. Just a small, battered blue car.

Well, shit.

I take a quick glance to the west. The sun is murky at best through those clouds, and once it slips past the edge of the mountain, unfortunate hikers could end up here all night. Especially since rain is coming, and that always turns newbies upside down and sideways.

I jump out and begin striding down the trail. Talking to strangers is just about my least favorite activity, but I can't leave anyone stranded out here. Which seems to happen every couple of weeks, dammit.

"Hellooo..." I bellow down the trail. No response, other than from a few annoyed birds and squirrels. I take off at a slow jog toward the edge of the ridge. From there anyone in the area should be able to hear my holler.

After a few minutes, I stop short and look down. Three sticks are in a distinct line at the edge of the trail, pointed west. It's a marker.

Peering into the brush, I hear shuffling. Then something that sounds like a soft whimper.

I hurry toward the sound, hoping like hell that I'm not about to startle two half-naked teenagers. (That happened to me once last summer. And twice to my younger brother, Baz. You'd think it would be hilarious. No. It was extremely awkward.)

My boots are relatively quiet on the damp leaves as I trudge up the slight hill and look around. A spot of neon yellow catches my eye. Well, at least whoever this is was smart enough to wear something high visibility.

I pass a clump of trees, walk around a massive boulder,

and find myself standing in front of someone sitting on the damp ground.

My heart stops.

I'm floating. My ears are buzzing.

She's *breathtaking*.

The sweet face of an angel, surrounded by a halo of rich chestnut hair, topped off with a neon yellow beanie.

The girl looks up at me, her eyes wide and mouth open. Oh crap, she's probably terrified of me.

"It's okay."

Mom always reminded me to soften my low rasp around women, because I sound rough and aggressive, even when I'm happy as a clam. It's just the way my voice comes out. "I'm here to help," I say as gently as possible.

She smiles slightly. Is it weird that I can feel it in the center of my chest?

"Hi." Her voice is scratchy, and she makes a face as she clears her throat. "Sorry. I was yelling for help, and I think I've trashed my voice."

I approach very slowly, knowing that a guy more than twice her size might ring some alarm bells with her. Then I notice her right foot. "You're hurt." I drop to my knees. The top of her canvas shoe is torn, and her foot is obviously bleeding.

"I don't think it's really as bad as it looks," she whispers throatily. "Maybe if you could just help me back to my car?"

The light is quickly becoming dimmer. "We need to hustle. I'll carry you."

Reaching out my arm carefully, I watch her eyes to make sure it's okay for me to touch her. She seems glad of my help, and I slip my arm around her back and pull her to standing on her left foot.

She's clutching a camera bag along with a small

shoulder bag. Scouring the area around where she was sitting, I see nothing but the usual leaves and sticks.

"What are you looking for?" she asks.

"Trash."

She shakes her head firmly. "I never litter. Especially not in the forest."

I grunt in approval. "I'll take those." Swinging both bags over my shoulder, I scoop her up into my arms and begin walking toward the trail.

"Thank you."

My heart lurches from holding her pretty little face mere inches from mine. Everything about her draws me in...her full pink lips...bright, curious eyes...the way she seems to be analyzing me.

"I'm Sage."

"Barrett."

She smiles, and I have to tear my eyes away from her face. Sage is so damn pretty that it's hard to focus, and holding such a soft, graceful young lady in my arms is making certain body parts of mine react rather suddenly.

Looking down, I see another arrangement of three sticks. "Those your trail markers?"

"Yes." She smiles at me so hard I have no choice but to meet her wide blue eyes for a second. "And no, don't worry, I didn't break them off a tree or anything. I try to go by that 'leave no trace' mantra."

Returning to the actual trail, I can feel myself smiling. I'm shocked at myself. I just don't *have* this kind of reaction with anyone. People in general are too loud, too intrusive, and too chaotic. They rarely know what the hell they're doing, and they often end up messing things up for those of us who just want some peace and quiet and to be left the hell alone.

Yet this sweet girl is igniting something deep within me. Something new.

Picking up a gorgeous, fascinating girl and taking her back to my house to make her dinner?

Check and mate.

3

SAGE

I only realize it's started raining hard when we step onto the main trail. Maybe I shouldn't be clinging to Barrett like this, but I think having my arms around his neck is helping him to hold me steady. Who am I kidding? He could easily carry three of me.

It feels incredible to be wrapped in his arms. Comforting, of course. It's a huge relief to think that I won't be stranded deep in the woods. Yet this prickling heat is... I'm not even sure what. It's brand new, and feels...special.

I tuck my face into his shoulder when raindrops start falling into my eyes. Barrett doesn't seem to notice them. His thick eyebrows are kind of like awnings that block the water.

"Next time you're out, remember to set an alarm for an hour before sunset." His rich voice rumbles in his huge chest, making me smile against the flannel.

"I set one for half an hour before. But I didn't realize—"

"The mountain cuts off the light. Everyone forgets that." He looks down at me with what might be a glimmer of a smile in his eyes, but not his lips. "Always lie to yourself about time out here. You'll need more than you think."

Nodding, I grin. "Good idea. Thanks."

"Your trail markers were smart. It's how I found you."

I allow myself to feel pleased with myself as he carries me out to the edge of the parking lot, ducking under a maple to shield us. Without any trees to filter the rain out here, the water is pounding down. My car looks like it's sunk several inches into the mud.

He takes in the battered car, and frowns deeply. "You're not driving that little toy vehicle on these roads in the rain." He says the word "vehicle" like something is caught in his throat. "Where are you staying? I'll drive you."

"Oh. Um..." He stares at me until I have to say something. "I'm sleeping in my car this week. It's not so bad."

There's a heavy sigh, and he turns toward his huge gray truck. "You'll stay with me. I have to disinfect your foot."

He says it like it's a done deal. Like I don't have any say in the matter. It's clearly the right thing to do, though. He bundles me into his truck, grabbing a blanket from behind the bench for me.

"What do you need from your car?"

I hand him my keys. "Just the blue duffel bag in the back seat. Thank you."

Barrett grabs my bag, then jumps into his truck. I'm still shivering despite the blanket, and he turns the heat on full blast. Then he freezes, examining my eyes. "Are you... Are you afraid of me?"

I shake my head, my damp bangs pasted to my forehead.

There's a low grinding sound in his throat. "I can take you into town instead, to the clinic if you like. But my place is closer and I can fix your foot faster. Feed you, too."

"Your place would be great, thank you."

He nods, then pulls out onto the road. The forest is beautiful; the heavy rain is bringing out the deep greens in the low light, and making every leaf and needle glisten. If I weren't chilled to the bone, I'd open the window to breathe it all in.

We drive for several minutes, and then, out of nowhere, Barrett speaks again. "Mom always says my voice scares people off. Especially women. I sound mean." He glances at me with a strange expression. I can't be sure, but I think it's his way of saying that he doesn't want to frighten me.

"I'm not scared. You're sweet to take care of me." He snorts. "Well, sweeter than the bear who would have come to take care of me in a few hours?"

He actually chuckles. "Fair enough."

After a while, he turns off the road and the truck strains slightly to make it up the long gravel driveway. Barrett doesn't seem concerned, though, so I stay quiet until we round a corner.

"Wow," I breathe. "It's beautiful."

The large wooden house is designed in a classic cabin style, with a massive wraparound porch and huge windows facing the valley.

Barrett's jaw tightens, his bottom lip twitching with...is it pride?...as he glances at me sideways. "Built it myself," he finally mutters as we pull up in front. He grabs my bags. "Stay put." He takes everything inside, and several lights go on. Then he returns to scoop me into his arms, carrying me straight to the couch.

He slips off my left shoe, then carefully unties the right. His deep, woodsy eyes lock on mine. "I'll need to take this off to disinfect the cut."

My bottom lip begins to tremble, but I keep my mouth pressed closed, nodding.

"I'll try to minimize the pain."

I nod again, then gasp as he slips off my shoe and sock at once. A cringing shiver runs through me from the sting.

"Shit," Barrett mutters, scowling down at my bloodied foot. "Looks deep. Don't move."

As he hurries to the kitchen, I look around the house to distract myself from the pain. The living room, dining area and kitchen is all one big open concept space, done in earth tones and filled with beautiful natural wood. I spy a large herb garden sitting in pots on the dining room windowsill.

Barrett returns with a bowl of hot water and bathes my foot carefully. It hurts, but it's not torture. Once the blood is washed away, he nods. "Good. Not as deep as I thought."

He meets my eyes. "Your choice, Sage. If you want to walk on this, you should probably get two or three stitches."

A deep shudder runs through me, and it takes all of my strength to hold back a whimper. I can't even pretend to be brave anymore.

Barrett's deep eyes soften. "I have medical training. I'm very good. I'm guessing you don't like 'em?"

My head shakes emphatically. "Stitches on the back of my other leg as a kid," I force myself to whisper. "Please... I can't."

He pats my knee gently, his eyes softening even more. "If you promise to stay off it for a few days, I can do a pressure bandage, and we'll check it tomorrow."

I think for a minute, appreciating that he's both taking charge and letting me make my own decisions.

"I don't want to be a burden." My voice is still hoarse. "If you'd like me to leave tomorrow, maybe you should stitch me up."

His hand gently squeezes my knee, as a slight smile touches his eyes. "You're interesting, Sage. I wouldn't mind having you around for a few days. Plus..." He trails off, then chuckles sheepishly. "You know those fancypants meals you enjoy, but it feels stupid to cook them for just one person? If I have company, it's an excuse to make those."

Grinning, I place my hand over his and squeeze back. "I'll happily be your excuse to make fancypants meals. I've never had a wild mountain man cook for me before, thank you."

He opens a sterile pad, then frowns at the open bottle that smells like an entire hospital. "This'll sting like hell, sorry."

Before I can think of a clever retort, my mouth falls open in a silent scream as the antiseptic surges over my jagged cut.

"Go ahead and curse. Studies have shown that it actually helps."

I respond with a flurry of breathless, muttered cusses. I probably sound like a nun compared to his idea of cursing, yet even through the searing pain, I still want him to think I'm a nice girl.

"Well done...for a start." He winks, then gently fans the liquid with his hand to speed up the drying process while I stifle a gasp.

His gentleness feels incredible. He's so close that I can feel his warm breath on my ankle. A shiver runs up my spine as I wonder what it would feel like if he were breathing like that along my throat. Or against my lips. *Oh, my...*

He taps my big toe, staring at my blue-gray nail polish. "Don't girls go for pink and red anymore?"

I laugh at his distraction technique. "I was in a cloudy mood, I guess."

Barrett looks up and nods. "*Hmmf.* I understand those."

His thick fingers move quickly and surprisingly deftly,

cleaning the cut and covering it carefully in a sterile bandage. Then he wraps an elastic strip around my entire foot. "That might start to ache in an hour," he says. "Tell me and I'll loosen it."

"Okay." I grab his hand, making him look straight at me. "Thank you, Barrett. Really."

The slight twinkle in his eyes warms my heart. "You're welcome. We'll fix your throat next."

He lifts me so that I'm lying on the couch with my foot propped up on a pillow. Then he heads to the kitchen for a few minutes, returning with a steaming mug that he sets on the coffee table beside me.

Then he pauses. "Damn, I put a splash of whisky in that without thinking. How old are you?"

"Twenty-one."

"Good."

He returns to the kitchen and I watch as he putters around. The space is clearly designed for his size. I would have thought that a man that big would be sort of lumbering, yet his movements are as quick and efficient as when he was bandaging me up.

I sip the hot liquid gratefully. It's some sort of lemon-herb concoction that tastes odd, but not entirely unpleasant. And it does feel good on my throat.

Barrett starts pulling things out of the fridge, then glances over to me. "You aren't vegetarian, or have a thousand food allergies?"

"Nope, I'll eat anything," I smile. "Wait... You're not about to roast a squirrel or anything weird, right?

He actually smirks. "Fresh out of squirrels. Maybe tomorrow."

I've never watched a gorgeous man cook before. It's actually quite calming. Barrett is clearly not a very chatty guy, and grouchy seems to be his default setting, but a few basic questions are probably okay. "So, um, what do you do out here?"

His head cocks slowly to the side. "You mean for money? I own this big chunk of land, and have some investments. I've been very fortunate."

He fills a pot of water, waiting in silence before speaking again. I get the impression he's not accustomed to talking about himself much.

"Every day there's a lot to do. Work on the house. The truck. I make furniture in the workshop. Lots of maintenance on a property this size. Clearing dead trees and stuff." He turns to me and raises an eyebrow. "Lucky for you, a few of us take turns checking for cars at the trailhead at sunset."

"Like a volunteer squad?" I grin.

He snorts. "Sure. My younger brother Baz, my buddy Jace, a few other guys that drive by that parking lot on a semi-regular basis..."

"I really do appreciate it." I try to flash him my most winning smile. I'm desperate for this guy to like me. Not just because I'm apparently staying here for a bit. I feel drawn to him in a way I've never experienced before.

"Am I going to need to call a tow truck to get my car out?" My voice is a bit stronger already.

He shrugs, chopping something as quickly and methodically as if he were a professional chef. "Depends on how hard it rains overnight. I'll call Griffin the towing guy if my truck isn't up to it. No stress."

I'm not sure what else to ask him, so I sip my drink quietly and watch Barrett cook. He's a strange man. Super quiet, but he obviously has a good heart if he keeps an eye out for hapless hikers, and takes in a little stray like me.

I realize that on some level I should be nervous about

staying with a complete stranger. But for some reason, I'm not. I can already tell that Barrett is a good man through and through. He's just a grump who's had too many cloudy moods.

As the rain pours down outside, pattering against the roof and a huge front window, I make up my mind. I'm going to find a way to be his little ray of sunshine, and see if he'll let me into his world.

At least...for a day or two.

4

BARRETT

Thank goodness that Sage decided against me giving her stitches tonight. She'll be fine without them, because I'm not letting her take a single step on that adorable little foot for the next few days.

If it had been just a bit deeper, though, I might've not had a choice.

It was difficult to keep my hands from shaking when I touched her. I've never been so head over heels out of my mind for a woman before. But she's like a gorgeous little pixie who appeared in the forest to light up my life. I can't help it.

I'm grateful that I was there to find her, and that she is letting me take care of her while she heals. *Caring for Sage...* A tremor runs through me as I stir the pasta. Doing that full-time would pull my whole life together. Give me purpose. Help me channel and focus my energy.

Well, if I want to have a shot at that, I'm going to have to force myself to talk a lot more than usual. I'm the furthest thing from an expert when it comes to women, but I do know they're into communication. Which probably means more than just a few grunts and meaningful looks.

I set the table while everything simmers, then go over to see that Sage has finished her hot toddy. "Throat better?"

"Quite a bit, yeah. Thank you." Her voice is soft, but a bit of the raspiness is gone already.

I pick her up and carry her to the table, making her giggle. "Why do I feel like a fairy princess being waited on?"

Because you are a princess. I one hundred percent cannot say that. Let's go with...

"Wounded tiny girl privileges." I prop her foot up on the chair next to her and make sure everything is in easy reach. Then I plate the spinach and apple salad, and the beef and pepper rotini with freshly grated Parmesan Reggiano.

"The fancier stuff requires hours of marinating," I explain, sitting down to her left. "So tonight it's just squirrel... I mean beef."

Sage's laugh sounds like a sprinkling of fairy dust in the air around us. She reaches out and gives my forearm a feather-light smack. It thrills me to know she's already comfortable enough to touch me casually.

We begin to eat, and she rolls her eyes in bliss. "Oh wow, this salad dressing. Where did you find it?"

I point to the row of pots in the window. "Fresh herbs. Mince, throw 'em in olive oil for two days, then add some balsamic vinegar. Good as any restaurant I've ever been to."

Her radiant smile is utterly gorgeous. "A talented chef, a woodsman, *and* a medic? You really are the whole package."

I shrug. "Man's gotta take care of things."

After a few minutes of eating in silence, I realize I need to get her chatting again. "So, Sage, why were you out on Maple Trail?"

"I was taking photos for my blog."

I can't stop the growling grunt from escaping my throat. "One of those pretty-girl-prancing-around-in-nature things?"

She laughs, shaking her head. "No, that's not me at all. Just nature stuff – birds, animals, trees, flowers. Sometimes stones. Occasionally snails, butterflies, those chunky caterpillars." Her fork traces a slow circle on the plate. "I've been sending a whole bunch of my photos to different stock photography websites. I've only made a couple of sales so far, but I hope things will pick up."

"I bet they will." *Like you have any idea what you're talking about.* "Trends come and go. Maybe some ad campaign will suddenly need tons of chunky caterpillars."

"Maybe." Her head drops. "I slipped and tore up my foot because I was chasing a blue winged warbler."

"The little yellow guys?"

"Yeah. He had this amazing white triangle on his shoulder that was so perfect it didn't look real."

Nodding, I realize I'm smiling...*smiling*...as I look deeply into Sage's gorgeous blue eyes. "Think I've seen a couple of them with that marking. Must be hereditary. Family of them or something."

Her eyes light up. "Really? I'd love to get some more shots of them."

Absolutely not, I want to say. The thought of her getting hurt or stranded again is deeply upsetting. In fact, thinking about Sage being the slightest bit uncomfortable has my skin crawling and my shoulders tightening.

"I'd like to ask why you're sleeping in your car," I begin tentatively. "Unless that's none of my business."

She sighs, then takes a sip of water. "It's my older brother Carl's car, kind of. Well, we're supposed to share it equally. It was the last thing Mom gave us before she took off. I have some friends that run a daycare in Mackton – do you know that town?"

I nod. "Few hours west, just before Oakton?"

"Yeah. So I've been living there, and Carl's been using the car for..." Sage shivers. "His business stuff. I convinced him to let me have the car for a week twice a year so that I can go on photo safaris."

"And you sleep in the car?"

"It's like camping, since I can't afford a tent or anything. I was lucky to find a secondhand sleeping bag."

For a split second, I think of all of the extra camping gear I could dig out of the basement for her. Then reality hits me.

I don't want Sage to leave. Ever. If she's out there in the world without me to take care of her, what might happen?

"That's a pretty serious frown," she whispers. "Did I make you mad?"

My hand darts out to cover hers. "No. Just can't stand the thought of you out there in the cold alone."

Her twinkling eyes light up many parts of me at once. My heart, that I've ignored for a long time. My mind, that realizes I am truly enjoying chatting with her.

But also, my libido that I've pretty much ignored for ages.

My little forest pixie is the sexiest woman I've ever known.

Yeah, I'm already thinking of her as mine.

5

SAGE

I wake up slowly, and it takes me a moment to realize I'm not curled up uncomfortably and a little chilly in a sleeping bag in the back seat of my car.

Instead, I'm sprawled across a massive bed. As I try to roll over, my foot feels heavy. Oh, right...it all comes back now... Barrett insisted on slipping my foot into a spare pillowcase and pinning it to the sheets so I wouldn't thrash it around in my sleep.

He also insisted that I take the bed while he made do with the couch. I felt terrible about that, and honestly, I bet I would've slept even better with his huge warm bulk snuggled up right beside me, but it's beyond sweet that he wanted to be a gentleman.

Barrett genuinely seems to care for me. I don't think he'd act like this with just any hiker he found injured in the forest, would he? The idea gives me a strange special glow that makes me feel as alive and grounded as when I'm surrounded by pine trees.

When he was tucking me in, he managed to find every excuse to touch me, without ever once crossing a line. My heart flutters at the thought of how badly I want him to ignore those lines, stop being a gentleman, and do whatever he wants with me already.

I'm not sure why he's holding back, unless it's because I haven't been super clear that I want him. But I don't know how to do that. How do you flirt with a guy as solid as a mountain? I don't want him to think I'm a silly girl. He's already waiting on me hand and foot as if I'm some kind of helpless child. Not super alluring.

Carefully sitting up, I swing my feet over the side of the bed. My right foot immediately begins to throb. It's probably just from more blood rushing to it, but it's seriously sore.

Barrett thoughtfully left me an old canoe paddle to use as a crutch, so I hobble to the bathroom without putting any more than a shred of weight on the injury.

I wash up as quickly and quietly as possible, then change into a green sundress covered in a cute leaf pattern. Since I won't be hiking today, I might as well wear something comfortable. Plus, it's definitely more feminine.

After I brush my hair and swipe on a bit of tinted lip balm, I hop my way out to the kitchen as quietly as possible. Great, now *my* nickname is Hoppy.

Then I gasp, almost dropping the canoe paddle to the ground with a clatter.

Barrett is facing the huge dining room window, wearing nothing but a pair of black boxer briefs. It's the most unbelievably majestic and sensual vision I've ever taken in.

His back is... Well, he would be right at home in a bodybuilder competition. In fact, he'd probably win. His legs are like sculpted tree trunks. And that *ass*... I can't tear my eyes away completely, but instead of his butt I look back up at his shoulders and the rippled lines of his arms.

Barrett is freaking *hot*.

I must have made a noise, because he turns to see me standing awkwardly in the middle of the room.

Then he turns a bit more, and I see he's holding a coffee mug. He takes in my dress, then smiles with such sweetness that I'm taken aback. Wow. So gorgeous, with his eyes sparkling in the morning light.

But in a blink his expression switches to a frown. Yep, frowny and grumbly is definitely his default setting.

He sets down his coffee mug, rushing over to carry me to the dining room table. "Shoulda hollered for me to come get you." His voice is extra gruff first thing in the morning. It's maybe a little naughty, but I can't help but rub my cheek against his shoulder as he sets me down.

"I figured you needed your sleep."

"What I need is for you to heal." His eyes twinkle. "Voice sounds better, though. How's the foot?" He's already propping it up on a chair and examining the bandage.

"I think it's fine. It throbbed a bit when I first stood up, but that's just because the blood flow changed, right?"

"Probably."

He takes off the elasticized bandage and examines the dressing. "No bleeding. The slight swelling is going down. I'll take another look this afternoon." He wraps the bandage a bit looser this time, which definitely feels better.

My hand reaches out, and I can't stop my fingertips from trailing lightly over the huge swirls of ink around his left bicep.

"Damn," he mutters. "Sorry, I'm not dressed."

He walks casually to the bedroom, returning in a moment wearing a pair of dark but worn jeans and a fitted black t-shirt. I don't think he was even embarrassed, just concerned about being proper.

"But now I can't see the entire piece," I pout, staring at the partly covered ink on his arm.

Barrett actually grins, pushing up his sleeve on that side. "Better?"

"Yes. Thank you."

As he walks by me, his hand trails casually across the back of my shoulders. "Now, how do you take your coffee, and do you like scrambled eggs with rosemary and spinach?"

"Just a splash of milk, and that sounds amazing, thank you."

While Barrett prepares breakfast, I get him telling me about his herb garden, and the salad garden he has out back. For a few minutes he gets downright chatty, explaining about the importance of fresh greens, and how one should minimize the time between food being picked and being eaten to maximize their micronutrients.

"Plus," I say, waving my hand toward the tidy row of terracotta pots, "they are amazing decorations."

Barrett sets a plate of eggs down beside my steaming coffee. "Decoration? Look in the mirror." His eyebrow quirks up. "But of course a girl named Sage would look incredible in green."

My heart sings as I watch him plate his own breakfast. I notice he sits a bit closer beside me this morning. That's got to be a good sign.

"You call your brother to let him know you're okay?" he asks.

"Um..." I'm not quite sure how to say it. "No. He doesn't check in with me like that. He'll send me a text in a few days when we're supposed to meet to get the car back to him."

A strange sound that's a cross between a grunt and a growl emanates from Barrett's huge chest.

"I'm sorry," I say automatically. "I don't have to stay here until then. If you could maybe just drive me back to my car, I could—"

"No." He sighs heavily, then grows silent for a moment. "I don't want you to leave. I also don't want you to have a brother who doesn't sound like he gives a shit."

What do you say to that? "Oh."

His hand covers mine tentatively, as if he half expects me to pull away. "I don't like the idea of you not having..." He hesitates. "Backup. Someone you can rely on. I'm not saying that you're not a strong, independent young lady. But everyone needs help sometimes."

"You clearly don't," I say with a smile, which makes him lighten up a bit.

"Not true. When I was building this house, I called in a bunch of friends. There were plenty of times when I wasn't sure if one pair of hands would've been enough."

"I'm glad to hear that you have friends, but your stoic loner mountain man vibe is totally destroyed. Now I'm picturing you throwing fancy cocktail parties here every summer."

He harrumphs, but his eyes are smiling. "Cocktail parties? Not likely. My limit is having a handful of guys over to watch the playoffs and have a few beers."

"Did you serve fancypants hors d'oeuvres?"

"Just bowls of chips. Wait... I added fresh chives and oregano to some store-bought dip. Fancypants enough?"

"Plenty."

When our plates are clean, I automatically start to stand up, but a heavy hand lands on my shoulder. "Where do you think you're going?"

I stick out my bottom lip and try to imitate his grumbling demeanor. "I wanted to help with the dishes."

"No."

I attempt a growl, which only makes Barrett chuckle. "Look, I appreciate you taking care of me, but I'm really not used to being waited on like some kind of—"

"Princess?" His hand reaches out slowly, again as if expecting me to flinch. He cups my cheek, his thumb running along my cheekbone. "You are kind of like a princess. But also a little forest sprite from the woodland stories."

That's the sweetest thing anyone's ever said to me, and again I don't know how to respond.

"Dishes can wait. Health and healing first."

I make a chirp of surprise as Barrett picks me up, carrying me to the door and kicking it open gently. He sits on the porch bench with me in his lap, both of us facing the sun. "This all right?" he asks gruffly. "You need vitamin D and fresh air...as long as you're warm enough?"

My left arm is around the back of his shoulders, and my hand instinctively starts playing with the back of his hair. "This is great, thank you. And thanks for breakfast – everything was delicious."

It's not just that our bodies are pressed together. More importantly, I feel very close to Barrett emotionally. I feel like he's letting his guard down and wants to allow himself to be closer to me.

"I'm still pissed about your brother." His low voice sends rumbling twitches through my stomach. "You should be cared for. You're so sweet, Sage. Like those cute little birds you like to photograph."

I snicker. "You think I'm a bird?"

"No. Well, at first glance, yes, kind of cute like a bird. But then..." His right hand runs gently up and down the length of my back as the left reaches out and begins to stroke my cheek. His hands say more than his words. He likes me. He thinks I'm sexy. So why the hesitation?

Then it hits me. He's trying to be proper again.

"Hey," I whisper. "If you're trying to do the right thing and make sure that the injured, stranded girl doesn't feel trapped with you, I appreciate it. But..." I can feel myself blushing furiously, but force myself to spit it out. "I am completely open to you kissing me right now, if that's what you're thinking about. Just sayin'."

His beautiful hazel eyes hold mine, as if in a trance.

Then he moves slowly, leaning in gradually, giving me every opportunity to change my mind. I tip my head up and our lips meet in a feather-soft kiss that takes my breath away.

It only takes about twenty seconds for the gentle, delicate kiss to become much deeper. Hotter.

Then I hear a soft growl in his throat. Is it a warning that things are about to get even more interesting? Or a promise?

6

BARRETT

I'm surrounded by nature all day, every day, and it invigorates me. Yet I've never felt as alive as the second Sage's lips met mine.

She kisses like a dream – soft and warm and perfect. It ignites every savage, animalistic urge I've ever had.

I need to claim her. Want to possess her. Have to obsess over every soft inch of fair skin, every touch and caress of her perfect, sexy body. She's the dream girl I wasn't ready to fantasize about. Yet here she is in my arms, in my home, and she's all mine.

For a few days, at least.

I can't think about any of that yet. All I can do is kiss her harder as her lips part, encouraging me to delve even deeper. Her fingers thread through the back of my hair, telling me that she wants more. Gliding my tongue against hers feels like a gift. Like we're bonding. Like we're opening up to each other.

My hands run all over her back, her waist, her hips. Then I stroke down the outside of her thigh. Hitching up the skirt of her sundress a bit to reveal her bare skin, I trail my fingers gently around her knee, then the back of it.

Sage giggles against my lips. "Ack. That tickles."

I respond with a groan, caressing her calf, then her outer thigh. My entire body aches to lift her and take her straight to the bedroom so I could examine every ticklish nook and delicious curve.

But taking my time with her feels...important, somehow. Even though I might only have her for a few more days.

Sage sighs as she sinks into our kiss, her fingers clutching me hard as if she never wants to let go.

"Princess," I murmur against her soft lips, "tell me to stop."

"Mmm...no."

I tilt my head the other way, keeping her close, holding back a groan as the kiss takes on a life of its own. A deep, primal craving is being unleashed inside me, and holding it back is going to be a challenge. Twisting slightly, I fight to keep her just far enough away that she doesn't feel my throbbing erection.

She pulls back with a start. "I'm so sorry. Do you have to go? Do you have work to do?"

"You apologize much too much." My nose brushes against hers until she giggles. "I deserve a day off. Besides, right now my most important job is taking care of you."

Her eyes grow wide as she blinks sharply. Has nobody ever spoken sweetly to this precious girl before?

"Don't be sorry, princess. You're not a bother."

She shrugs with an exasperated sigh. "Except that I *am*. Here you are, letting me stay here for free, and I can't even cook for you."

"You can tell me all about your life while I marinate some chicken." I bounce her slightly on my knee. "And if you're really lucky, I'll let you shred the lettuce for our lunch salad. How's that?" Her smile lifts her cheekbones. Analyzing this sweet face will be my mission every second she's near me.

"It's great that you eat so healthy."

"You think a grumpy loner bachelor should be living on frozen dinners and pizza?"

"No. I guess I've just never thought about it."

My thumb glides along the silky skin of her cheek. "Food is fuel. I'm always busy. Cars run better when there's quality gas in the tank."

Sage nods. "Mechanically minded. Got it."

Lifting her carefully, we go inside and I sit her on the kitchen counter so she can lean back against the cabinets. I ask Sage questions as I start the marinade for the chicken.

I adore the way she chatters away so brightly once she gets going, but I'm starting to read between the lines. Her mother was clearly neglectful even before she took off, although Sage is too kind to come out and say it. And I *hate* the furrow in her brow whenever she mentions her brother and his "business".

It's clear Carl sometimes takes Sage with him as a decoy and a cover when he's making his deliveries. Aside from that, he ignores her most of the time, except when he's controlling her. It makes my fists clench and jaw tighten just to think about it. The thought of anyone using Sage makes me physically ill.

Although...I don't even want to go there...I'm kind of controlling her as well. Sure, I'm using the logic that it's in her best interest to stay off her foot for several more days to heal and be safe, whereas Carl is clearly manipulating her for his own benefit. And yet...hmm.

The longer she stays with me, the more comfortable she

might become. The more she might feel at peace in this house. Feel healthy and happy while living out here in the forest. Feel secure in this incredible connection between us.

It's not being manipulative if I'm positive it's great for us both...right?

7

SAGE

I've never thought about what kind of guy I'd like to end up with someday – maybe because the examples of manhood I've had up till now have been pretty lousy.

Dad took off when I was seven. I've tried really hard to have neutral feelings about my brother – we're supposed to be helping each other out – but now that I see him through Barrett's eyes, there's no way to varnish the truth anymore. Carl is, frankly, a loser, and I suspect he's into some really shady things.

Luckily, Barrett doesn't pry into that. It does, however, feel like he's genuinely trying to be more chatty, and we spend a fantastic day with him cooking and me assisting whenever possible. By the time he carries me to the couch after dinner, there's no denying it anymore: we want each other.

His phone vibrates for the first time all day, clattering slightly on the coffee table. "Sorry," he mutters.

"No problem. Anything important?"

He glances at the screen, shaking his head. "Just my

brother Baz. A bunch of us are getting coffee next week to figure out a solution to the tourist problem."

"Tourist problem?"

He pushes the phone aside, then pulls me so that I'm sitting with my legs over his lap. This way I can either lean back against the arm of the couch, or cuddle into his shoulder. Naturally, I choose his shoulder. It still seems like he wants to be extremely careful with me. Me, I want to give him clear signals that maybe he doesn't have to.

"The town council of Old Hemlock Valley is meeting in a few months about bringing in more tourists. Which is fine, but we want them to be careful about who they target."

"You only want the right kind of tourists?"

"Exactly." Barrett frowns, somehow grumbling without making a sound.

"You hate tourists that much?"

He looks at me carefully. "Not all of them. Just the disrespectful ones."

"Like the ones who litter."

"Yeah. Or the ones that tear bunches of leaves off the trees for some craft project. The ones who don't come prepared with any supplies or protective gear. Don't get me started on the morons who make a fire in the middle of the forest with no idea what they're doing, just for some dumb video."

"So you don't want so-called influencers or content creators. You want actual nature lovers."

"Yeah."

"Birders!" I can't help but laugh at his look of confusion in response to my wide smile. "Seriously. They're always quiet and respectful, and they tend to read the rules before they go anywhere. They're big on research."

"That's the problem. On the public trails there are no official rules."

"Couldn't the town make them?" I stop staring at Barrett for a moment to look out the window at the darkening forest. "You can make a big sign right at the trailhead, on the gate. So that they have to walk right beside it to go by."

"Sure. But do people even read signs these days?"

"They might if you made it funny. Give them a hashtag to share their best photos. Bloggers love their hashtags. Oh, and maybe something about how you have to read the rules then high five the sign as a virtual signature before you're allowed entrance."

"Even if it's all on the honor system?" Barrett chuckles, nodding. "Well, I guess all it would cost us is a sign and a couple of nails." He threads his fingers through mine, then looks down at our hands. "You're very smart, Sage. I like that."

"And I like how dedicated you are to the forest." My fingers squeeze his. "It's very admirable. Sweet, even."

His head shakes, smiling ruefully. "You're the only person who has ever called me sweet besides my mother. And even then she was probably just being polite."

"Really?" Somehow I find the courage to walk my fingers up his shoulder to caress the back of his ear gently. "I think it's incredibly sweet that you cooked for me all day. Re-bandaged my foot. And that you're letting me stay here while I heal."

As soon as I say the words, I want to bite them back. The thought of leaving him and this place fills me with a strange, almost sickening sense of dread. Which is completely nuts, since we've just met, but I can't help it. Everything I feel about Barrett is more real and honest and natural than anything I've ever felt before.

"Sage." He faces me head on. "You're the sweet one. You deserve to get everything you want out of life."

He hesitates, and it's surprising and charming to see such a strong man looking slightly vulnerable. "Completely hypothetically, of course, princess – could you ever see yourself living in a tiny town on a mountain instead of in a city?"

"Definitely." My immediate, certain response lowers his shoulders half an inch.

"Good. Don't want to get my hopes up if there's zero chance." He stares so deeply into my eyes I feel like I'm falling. I love it. "These feelings. They're...new for me." His rough voice is even grittier. "Dunno what I'm supposed to say. But I need you to know that I want you. Not just while your foot heals. More. A lot more."

I'm already nodding. "I don't know what I'm supposed to say either. But we're on the same page."

"Good." His expressive eyes seem to make the few words he says more intense. "Now, my little birder, should I carry you to bed?"

My fingers grip the back of his hair snugly and I squint at him. "You'll stay with me, right?"

There's a faint clicking sound, which I think is his back teeth grinding. "I'll take the couch."

"No. You can't take the couch again," I sigh. "You can bounce back from one night of sleeping strangely. Two nights in a bad bed makes a person miserable."

"In case you hadn't noticed, I'm already miserable. Ask anyone."

"I don't think you're miserable."

His eyebrows raise sky-high. "Really?"

"Really. You're set in your ways, sure. Stoic. Quiet. That's fine." I grin. "You have some strong opinions about tourists, but only because you want to keep the forest pristine. I agree with that."

Again, he manages to grumble without making a sound.

"And... Mayyybe if you relaxed with me, you'd be less miserable?" I shift, bringing my hands to the front of his chest. "Your bed is huge. I really don't take up much room. Why not share? Then we'll both be comfy."

More clicking. "And if I reach for you in my sleep?"

"Then we snuggle. All good."

Suddenly I realize why he has me sitting on the couch with just my legs stretched across his lap. My knee is now brushing against a massive, rock-hard erection.

Fighting the urge to giggle, I'm touched by how much he wants to keep things respectable.

"I won't be offended." My hands gently circle the thick swaths of muscle across his chest as my knee *very* deliberately brushes against him. "You obviously like nature. It's natural for animals to cuddle for warmth, isn't it?"

A smile slowly spreads across his lips. "Saucy. Didn't know I liked that. Huh."

Barrett carries me to the bedroom, and I change in the bathroom. He's given me a t-shirt to wear as a nightgown that literally hangs to my knees. I love that he uses unscented laundry soap – there's nothing to compete with the smell of fresh cotton, the scent of the forest through the cracked open bedroom window, and the faint, masculine musk of my sexy mountain man.

I come back out and slip into bed, where I'm delighted to discover that he's wearing nothing but those snug-fitting boxer briefs. His broad, tanned chest and thick arms are savage and powerful in the dim light of the bedside lamp. He looks like a warrior. Timeless. Noble.

Maybe I should feel like a frightened jackrabbit near a

man this...virile. But I don't. We definitely want the same thing. Weird that he's more concerned about taking our time than I am.

But sweet.

Barrett matter-of-factly grabs my foot and loosens the elastic bandage a bit more. "Releasing the pressure gradually like this will increase the circulation and make sure your skin knits together well. I'll change the bandage again tomorrow."

"Thank you."

He massages around my heel, then my toes, avoiding the cut itself but bringing a bit of extra circulation to the area. "Wiggle those little cloudy toes for me." I wiggle obligingly. "No pain?"

"No. There's a slight...tension. Stiffness, I guess?"

"Good. Healing fine." He scrunches his face up, trying to look stern. "As long as you behave and stay off it."

I grin. "Yes, Mr. Medic, sir."

He tucks me carefully into the blankets, then fluffs up my pillow. At first I'm incredulous that he's so fussy, then I realize he's actually joking. My laugh seems to delight Barrett as I sweep my hair to the side and snuggle in beside him.

"If I hold you too tight, just shove me away," he murmurs. "You won't offend me if you need some space."

"Yeah. The same goes for you."

He grins, squeezing his arms around me gently. "Think I like you in my space."

"Good. I'm glad. But if you need to go work, or run errands, or need me to leave, just say—"

"No." The word is quiet, but forceful. "Stay as long as you like." His hand slides down to caress my hip, and I'm suddenly excruciatingly aware of how close his palm is to my underwear.

I can feel his hesitation, so I stay silent, encouraging him to speak again. He doesn't. Instead, he slowly pulls me against him. There's something subtly possessive about him moving my body instead of him leaning closer to me. It makes the center of my chest feel overheated. And between my legs. And...oh wow, *everywhere*.

I don't know where this is going to go. I don't know when Barrett is going to cross the line and stop being such a gentleman, but I hope it's soon.

Because I've never wanted a man like this. And I couldn't imagine a more caring guy to share my first time with.

No matter what happens.

8

BARRETT

My heart is racing. Fingers twitching. Cock throbbing like crazy as I keep shifting, trying to keep it from touching Sage.

She's so gorgeous, so perfect. I shouldn't be having these incredibly possessive feelings about her. This longing. This...*need.*

Not just a need to hear every tiny sound she makes as I thrust inside her. I need to feel her joy. Need to take care of her.

Maybe if I only touch her, and don't allow her to touch me, that will keep us from going too far too fast. I'm totally making up the rules as I go along, but I need to feel that I'm not rushing her.

"Sage, I need you to do something for me."

"Anything." I love how immediate her response is.

"I need you to clearly say the word 'stop'."

Her eyebrow quirks up, then her eyes soften. "And if I don't want to say it?"

I shake her hip slightly. "Just say it."

She grins. "Stop."

"There." I place our foreheads together. "Feel free to say that at any time, okay?"

"Okay. But I don't think I will."

This girl. A deep, grumbling groan echoes low in my throat.

Rolling Sage gently onto her back, I kiss her softly, wanting to be sure that she isn't nervous about having my body over hers. I don't want her to feel trapped, even though the feeling of possessing her is revving my lust to the limit.

She tries to wrap herself around me, clinging to my frame. Gently shoving up her t-shirt, I run my palm along her stomach and ribs. She kisses me deeply, her fingers threaded through the back of my hair.

It's obvious she wants more. A sense of responsibility for caring for this luscious girl washes through me. I've never shirked responsibility of any kind, even taking on much more than I should when it comes to patrolling the local trails, and helping neighbors. A man has to do his duty.

Well, now my duty is to make Sage feel incredible. Feel safe with me. Her health and comfort is now all on me.

Pushing her shirt up a little more, my rough palms skim across her tender breasts. Her breath becomes fluttery, sending a deep shudder down my spine. This precious girl has never been touched by another man, I can feel it. The wave of possession coursing through my veins feels like adrenaline mixed with molten steel.

My lips wander down her throat, skipping over the bunched-up t-shirt to circle lazily around her left breast. Her fingers tighten in my hair and she sighs the moment my lips clamp around her nipple.

Damn, I love how expressive she is. How easy to read. Sage guides me like her rows of sticks in the forest, telling me without words that she loves it when I touch her gently.

Slowly. How she loves feeling my thick fingers digging into her skin, grabbing her firmly as I scrape my teeth carefully across her pebbled flesh.

I switch to the other side, caressing and kissing her breast as my right hand slides down her stomach. "Remember that word you're supposed to say?" I rasp as my fingertips inch into the top of her panties.

"I have no idea what you're talking about." My head pops up for a moment to see her give me a saucy wink.

I groan as my fingertips make contact with her softest skin. Through a faint dusting of silky hair, I feel her silky lips, spreading them open to discover moisture. I didn't think my cock could get any harder, but knowing that Sage is wet for me makes it pulse in time with my heartbeat.

She begins to sway on the bed, as if she enjoys being pinned down by my much larger frame. I put a pillow under her injured foot to remind her not to move it around. I don't want my princess to be troubled with the slightest bit of pain. As her legs splay apart, I accept the silent invitation to run my blunt fingertip straight through her inner lips, teasing at her opening.

Her faint breathy moan makes my long-neglected heart swell.

My finger dances and twists, gently teasing before drifting slightly upward. Moving in slow, meandering circles, I explore the nub of her clit, watching the way her eyes grow hooded and heavy. Sucking her nipple hard enough to make her jump slightly, I lift my head to study her. It's like she's melting against me, warm and soft, giving in to every sensation.

My palm massages her pert breast as I run my teeth along her bottom lip. "You like it right here, princess?" My finger brushes straight across her clit as Sage's back arches, her breath coming in halting, stuttering gasps.

"Yeah." The harder and faster my finger circles, the more frantically her fingers rake through my hair, her nails pricking my scalp lightly.

"*Oh...*" she gasps, as I replace my circling finger with my thumb, pressing gently against her sensitive skin. This leaves the rest of my fingers free to explore her folds, dragging carefully across every pulse point as she begins to pant hard.

"Yes. Let go for me." My voice is too deep, too rough. I shouldn't scare her with such a command, yet it bursts out.

Sage's eyes light up. "Mmm..." she moans. "Say that again."

And something inside me snaps.

I need to get closer. I need to be as intimate with this gorgeous girl as I possibly can, without plunging myself inside her. At least, not that way. Not yet.

She moans when I pull away, then gasps as I pull her panties down one leg and shove them aside. I shift and settle between her soft thighs, my shoulders spreading her legs wide as I dive right in, kissing her beautiful pink pussy. I lick her as though I'm starving, dragging my tongue slowly around, then gently pushing inside her tender skin.

Sage gasps, her fingers gripping my hair just above my ears. Once she's nice and wet, I begin swirling my tongue around her clit. "Let go for me," I growl again.

"Oh!" Her soft gasps and moans are becoming erratic. My hand presses down on her hip bone to hold her steady, and my splayed fingers can feel the fluttering deep in her lower belly.

"Come on my tongue," I command, lapping straight

across her sensitive button as my thick finger slips inside her just enough to make her start to shake. "Let me feel it."

I hope that she can see in my eyes how much I need this. Need her pleasure. Her surrender. Her trust in me.

I groan deeply as she pulls my face right into her soft, wet pussy. Licking steadily, I watch her eyes grow wide, then she falls back with a soft, broken scream as the climax crashes through her. Her legs tense around my ears, her hands shaking, her perfect perky breasts bouncing.

I've never seen anything so gorgeous in my life.

As her quivering slowly subsides, I lick all around her pussy lips, drinking in her juices as if I want to absorb her sweetness. Then I sit up, looking around for her underwear to slip it back on.

Sage looks surprised, but stays quiet. I kiss each of her nipples in turn, then pull the t-shirt back down and throw the blankets back over us.

Once she's cuddled safely in my arms, I whisper, "You're so beautiful when you lose control."

She smiles, her fingers trailing slowly around my shoulder. "That was incredible. Thank you. There aren't even words."

Our lips meet so naturally, as if I was destined to kiss this girl for the rest of my life. I can already feel the magnetic pull. The need. To make her mine, not just for tonight, but forever.

Then she pulls away to examine my eyes. "Don't you want to... I mean, I could—"

"Easy, princess. It's our first night together."

I can't tell her that I would probably come in less than a minute if she simply ran her delicate palm up and down my aching cock. Can't tell her of the visions I'm having of the look in her eyes once I finally plunge my shaft into her.

Caring for my lovely girl will include making sure that she doesn't feel trapped with me.

In town, everyone thinks of me as the grump who avoids people. Out here in the middle of the forest, people know me as the rescuer. The good guy.

I'm not yet positive what kind of man Sage needs, but I'm prepared to be anything and everything for my princess.

9

SAGE

Barrett gives me the okay to take a quick shower this morning before he rewraps my foot, thank goodness. It makes me feel completely energized.

Watching him move around the kitchen after we're done breakfast, putting dishes away while another pot of coffee brews, is my new favorite form of entertainment. I can't get over how graceful he is. Maybe he's just lived here so long that he's learned the most efficient way to navigate the kitchen.

I've noticed that Barrett is efficient in most things, except for last night when he certainly took his time with me. Every time I think about that my belly flutters and my shoulders creep up an inch from the prickling sensation that instantly runs down my spine.

The way he touched me was so gentle, until I made it clear I needed more. He's so cautious with me. I've never had anyone in my life who is that caring.

Mom was nice to me sometimes, because she had to. But as soon as I was able to take care of myself, she was off like a shot. Meanwhile Carl is only nice to me when he wants something.

Barrett, though? He just wants me to be happy. I can tell already he doesn't have it in him to play games. Maybe it's naive for me to think that I know someone so well after just a few days, but I honestly think Barrett couldn't be more open.

He brings me a fresh cup of coffee, setting his own mug beside mine. Then his eyes crinkle up with that adorable half smile. I wonder if, from a distance, strangers see it as a scowl?

"May I see some of your photos? Your blog?"

"Sure," I say with a grin.

I start to get up, but he shoves my shoulder back down ever so gently. "No. I'll bring your camera bag."

"And my laptop, please – in my duffle bag."

Instead of just reaching in to grab the laptop, he brings me the entire bag, setting it on a chair beside me.

He seems surprised by my laughter. "I've heard that you guys were sometimes afraid to go into a woman's purse and rifle through her things. I didn't know it was true."

He scratches the back of his neck awkwardly. "Might be...girl things...you don't want me to see."

I gasp. "Barrett, are you actually blushing under that tan?"

He scowls. "*No.*"

"You are!" I tease.

There's a low growl from the back of his throat. "And here I thought you were a nice girl."

I can't help laughing even louder while I slip the memory card out of my camera and into the laptop. Turning it toward him, we flip through the photos I took the other day.

I keep quiet as he nods, murmuring the name of every bird, and pointing out some of the rarer species of trees.

"Maybe I should add some of those to my stock photo collections. I'm hoping to start making a little more money from my photos. Perhaps if I have photos of stuff that other people don't, it will help," I muse. Then I open my blog, turning it toward him so that he can scroll through a few pages' worth of posts.

He reads quickly, nodding in agreement with some of my points, and even chuckling once or twice. Then he turns to me with a dazzling smile. "I was worried about you going off the trail. But you're right – it was worth it for those photos."

He pushes the laptop back a bit and takes my hand. "You respect the forest. This is one of the good blogs. Informative, charming, and it's about your topic, not...well...yourself." His fingers squeeze mine gently as he looks deep in my eyes. "It's wonderful, Sage."

"Thank you." I'm touched that he likes it. "I get comments sometimes from people who live in cities saying they like to read my posts on coffee breaks so they can pretend they're out in nature."

Barrett's head tilts to the side as he stares down at our hands for a moment. "If your blog is focused on the birds and wildlife of Old Hemlock Valley, it could be useful for people who are planning to come hiking out this way."

"For sure. Real nature lovers."

"Maybe you could add a link to the town's tourism website. And they can link to your blog. Cross promotion or whatever it's called."

"Oh!" My mind is already racing. "Maybe I could speak with some naturalists in the area. Field researchers. Experienced hikers. People like you, who know the forest."

His eyebrows pull together. "You're not interviewing me."

"I wouldn't have to use your name. We could write a post sharing a few insider tips. The best seasons to see certain species, when is the best weather, that sort of thing."

"Safety information." Barrett nods. "A checklist of what they should have in their backpack before they even think about going out into the wilderness."

"Perfect."

I want to keep brainstorming, but just then my phone beeps from where it's charging in the bedroom. Barrett jumps to his feet and brings it to me face down, as if to make it abundantly clear that he's not even looking at it. Sweet.

I sigh. "It's my brother Carl." Skimming through his texts, apparently he wants me to give him the car back tomorrow. Something about an important deal, and needing to deliver some things. It makes me a bit queasy that he always expects me to drop everything to help him.

"Is he worried about you?" Barrett asks. "Did you tell him that you were hurt but you're healing quickly?"

"I, um, never mentioned it." It's sickening to realize that Carl truly doesn't care about me at all. I don't think he's ever once asked if I'm okay. Even though he knows that I drive out to hike alone, and always sleep in the car.

Crap. I still don't know if I'll have to get the car towed, or how long it might take to get to where Carl wants me to drop it off.

"I usually drive back to Mackton and he picks up the car. This time he needs me to drop it off in..." I peer at the screen again. "How far away is Pinesley?"

Immediately, Barrett's jaw clenches. "I don't want you going there." His voice has dropped, sounding even more gruff than usual.

"Um..." There's a squirming, heavy feeling in my stomach. I don't want Barrett to meet Carl, unkempt, uncouth, and frankly kind of rude as he is, for fear that my mountain man will think less of me.

"But to answer your question, it's about forty minutes southeast of here." His hand slides under the table, fingers tapping on his knee. Staring at the table for a full minute, it's like he's trying to burn a message into the wood with his eyes.

Finally he says, "If he hasn't mentioned what kind of business it is, it's nothing that a nice young lady should be anywhere near."

I'm still trying to figure out how to respond to that when there's a knock at the door which makes me jump a mile. A heavy hand lands on my shoulder, then gently caresses my neck. "Shh, Sage. It's probably just a neighbor."

He crosses the length of the house in just a few strides. "Come on in, Riggs."

A tall, burly man as big as Barrett steps in, glancing at me in obvious surprise. "Just brought your compressor back. It's on the porch. Should I put it in the garage for you?"

"Nah, that's fine. Riggs, this is Sage."

I wave and he nods. "Nice to meet you."

He's wearing dark worn jeans almost identical to Barrett's, but his snug t-shirt is dark gray instead of black.

"Riggs has a house around here, but he only drops by to borrow my tools." Barrett's gruff tone is softened by the way he throws me a wink that his friend can clearly see.

"Thanks for the loan," Riggs chuckles. "Ever need a favor, just holler."

"I do, actually." Barrett's eyes flick to me. "Could you run me down to the Maple Trail lot? If Sage's car isn't sunk too far in the mud, I'll drive it back."

"Sure thing."

"Thank you," I call out as Riggs gives me a nod and steps outside.

Barrett comes over to kneel beside me. "Perfect timing. Will you be okay by yourself for a bit?"

"Of course."

He carries me to the couch, making sure that I have fresh coffee, a glass of water, and the remote control.

He starts to leave, then pauses, glancing back at me almost sheepishly and pulling out his phone. "What's your number, princess?"

He shoots me a text, waiting to make sure my phone beeps from the coffee table.

"Back soon."

He stops at the door again, then looks back at me. He returns and drops to one knee, leaning in for a gentle, almost breathless kiss. His hand tangles in the back of my hair, holding me against him as I try not to quiver. Even his softest kiss manages to make me tingle all the way down to my toes.

"Better," he whispers. He kisses me one last time, then straightens up, winking again before he leaves.

After he's gone, the house feels achingly empty. Hollow. Even though he's so silent, Barrett is a huge presence.

I'm blown away that he left me here alone, although he barely knows me. I would never prowl around in his things, of course, but he doesn't know that. Well, he knows that I can't exactly prowl: I'd be hopping on my canoe paddle crutch. I don't know which would disappoint him more, the hopping or the snooping.

Already, we can read each other so well. Which is why I feel like a jerk for wanting to keep him away from Carl—

No. To be more accurate, I want to keep Carl away from *him*.

I send Carl a text, saying only that I'll be in touch tomorrow. I don't want to commit to anything more yet, since I have no idea what's going on there.

Not just with the car, either. Whatever Barrett and I have together is so new and fragile that I don't know how to navigate it. He's been tiptoeing around the thought of me staying for a while longer, even after my foot heals, but I don't know what he's thinking for the longer term. Does he want us to date? Surely he can't imagine I'd move in right away.

Staring out the window to the lush, green forest, I realize I have some decisions to make. And some questions that need answers.

First, how am I going to get the car to Carl when Barrett doesn't want me to go to Pinesley at all, and certainly not alone?

Second, do I want to stay here in Old Hemlock Valley? It would be a dream come true to not have a day job, and just be able to work full time on my photography, my blog, and promoting birding in this area.

And the biggest question of all: how do I figure out what Barrett's intentions are when he speaks so little and is the opposite of forthright about what he wants for the future?

10

BARRETT

Riggs isn't quite as quiet as I am. We barely make it to the end of the driveway before he asks, "So, is Sage the girlfriend?"

How the hell do I answer that honestly? She's not just "the girlfriend". She's...the *one*. My sweet, precious princess that I want to protect forever.

"Still very new," I say cautiously. "Hoping she'll stay."

Riggs waits until we're pulling into the Maple Trail parking lot before speaking again. "Have you actually *asked* her to stay with you? I don't claim to know a thing about women, but supposedly they appreciate clarity." He turns to give me an unconvinced shrug. "At least, that's what Hollywood says, right?"

I snort a chuckle. "I guess."

I jump out of the truck and unlock Sage's car, moving the seat back as far as it'll go to squash myself (barely) into it. Luckily it starts, but it complains a fair bit as I try to drive it out of the mud patch. Then I spot Riggs standing behind the car, nodding at me in the rearview mirror. I roll down the window and call out. "One, two, *three*."

He throws all his weight into it, giving enough of a shove that when I floor it, the car lurches out. I drive to the edge of the lot, then jump out. "Thanks, man."

Riggs shakes my hand. "Thank *you* for always sharing your tools." His expression lands halfway between a smile and a smirk. "Sage looked at you with what I think the romance writers call 'stars in her eyes'. The sooner you tell her how you feel, the easier I think everything will be."

"You sound like one of those women's talk show hosts," I grumble. Then I nod reluctantly. "But you're probably right. Thanks."

He claps me on the shoulder, then returns to his truck. He waits to make sure the car makes it out of the lot and onto the road before tapping the horn twice and driving off in the opposite direction.

At the next safe spot, I pull slightly off the road and grab my phone. I've never really texted women before, but Sage would probably like to know that I'm thinking about her. Wouldn't she?

Me: Hey, princess. Your car is way too small for me. But it's out of the mud. On my way home. Hope to find you on the couch right where I left you.

I'm not sure how long it normally takes a young lady to respond, but with this particular young lady it's under sixty seconds.

Sage: I might have raised and lowered my arm a few times while switching channels. That was the limit of my exercise. Thanks for saving my crappy car!

Damn, she's constantly funny and charming. A little ray of sunshine.

As I begin driving again, I can't help but wonder if a girl with such a sunny disposition belongs with a man who is as prone to cloudy moods as I am.

I want to be good for her. I need to convince her to stay with me. I'm already addicted to touching her, to hearing her stories. Just thinking of taking Sage on hikes to show her some new birds fills me with more happiness than I've had in a very long time.

Yet... What do I really have to offer her?

I groan to myself. I'm going to have to do exactly what Riggs suggested, and tell her how I feel.

Or, since I have no idea how to put that into words... Maybe I can show her.

11

____

SAGE

Barrett is a little different when he returns. Like he's forcing himself to be more talkative.

"Wow, that's one tiny car," he says, running his fingers affectionately through my hair on the way from the front door to the kitchen. "How would you like to have dinner on the porch tonight? Get you another dose of fresh air and all that. Like a picnic."

"Sure. Can I help?"

Instead of his usual scowl, his nose crinkles as he smiles slightly. "I'll think of something for you to do, don't worry."

A few minutes later, I've been hoisted onto the kitchen counter next to the sink and given the task of rinsing and tearing up spinach, then grating carrots for the salad.

"Salad wraps are great for hiking," he says as he grills the marinated chicken he started last night and stirs the coconut rice. "Just make a regular salad with less dressing, and throw it into a tortilla wrap. No cutlery, and just one sandwich bag or a small container."

"And you could eat it one-handed while you're walking, I'll bet."

"Exactly." He glances toward me. "You should never drop food in the forest, I'm sure you know that. But a few stray pieces of lettuce wouldn't be the end of the world."

It's only once we're out on the porch with the table set and he has draped a blanket around my shoulders that I realize what's happening. "Barrett," I ask softly, as the beautiful sunset reflects in his gorgeous hazel eyes, "is this a date?"

Instead of grumbling or growling, his face remains perfectly neutral for a few seconds. "Hope so." He reaches out to take my hand. "Sage, it's only been a couple of days, and you've kind of been trapped here with me..."

"I don't feel trapped at all."

"Well...good." His thumb caresses my hand gently. "You understand that I have feelings for you?"

I nod, my breath catching in my throat. "Yes. I hope you can tell I have feelings for you, too."

"Good." He's even more handsome when he smiles like that. His features are still rugged, but he's so sweet too. "Dig into that chicken while it's hot."

Over the next few hours, it feels like Barrett and I truly bond. It doesn't seem like a first date, more like our fourth or fifth. We enjoy the food, swap stories, and laugh a lot. I notice that Barrett is quick to scowl and grumble whenever I mention a rough point in my life. It's obvious that he hates that my mother took off on my brother and me. He also clearly can't stand that my brother has helped himself to the "shared" car most of the time.

It's interesting, though, that Barrett is very careful not to say anything blatantly negative about my brother. Perhaps he thinks he has a poker face, but I can see it in his eyes clear as day: he's genuinely upset at the thought of me being uncomfortable.

I've never felt so nurtured. It's also kind of oddly sexy that Barrett gets upset on my behalf. He's one hundred percent in my corner, which is a first for me. It's reassuring. Given time, I think this giant man could save me from my fears and negative thoughts, and quiet the constant voice in the back of my head that asks me if I'm really good enough.

Barrett definitely thinks that I'm good enough for him. *He wants me.* The knowledge sends tingling prickles through every muscle and nerve in my body. I just hope that tonight he'll let me touch him as well. Let me show him how I feel.

This time when I get ready for bed, I wear nothing but a long tank top that barely covers my butt. I also skip the underwear.

As soon as we snuggle together, Barrett's hand runs up my thigh and under my top to grip my hip. When he realizes there's nothing there, his grumble kicks in. "Forget something?"

"Didn't forget. Just didn't see the point."

Growl.

He kisses me suddenly, deeply, yanking my body hard against his. With my breasts pressed tight against his naked chest, I wonder if he can feel how fast my heart is beating. I gasp as the hard ridge of his cock presses against my mound. My hips automatically tilt against him, trying to create as much contact as possible.

"Sage." His voice is the dark scrape of steel against granite. "So fucking sexy. Been driving me crazy since the moment I saw you. How am I supposed to be a good man if you throw yourself at me like this?"

"Maybe I don't want you to be a good man. Just be yourself."

He kisses me even more fiercely until I can barely

breathe. When he rolls on top of me, his heat and weight surrounding me, my arousal rushes through my entire body.

I whimper in protest as his mouth leaves mine, then gasp as he shoves my tank top up to my collarbone so he can devour my breasts. Touching the back of his hair with one hand and his muscular shoulder with the other, my head is spinning.

"I love the way you touch me," I whisper. "The way you grab me."

"Know I should be gentle. Can't." He switches to the other side, his teeth lightly abrading my nipple until I shiver. I can feel my pussy growing wet and warm, and hope that he's finally going to take me.

His head ducks down, kissing a path across my belly, straight down between my legs as he shoves them wide open. Then he just stares for a moment, as if the sight of my naked flesh is making him crazy.

His arm scoops under my right thigh as he tilts my body up to his mouth. I love the way his eyes crinkle with a grin when I gasp at the way he licks and kisses, diving right in to devour my pussy as if he owns it.

Maybe he does. I already feel like I've given myself to him. We haven't said the words, but there's no mistaking this heat, this connection.

My mouth falls open with a shaky moan as his tongue plunges inside me. It's so unbelievably intimate. Even better, there's no hesitation whatsoever on his part as he grips me, caresses me, rubs his nose against my clit as his tongue thrusts deep.

Oh my... I'm going to come. I can feel the tension building in my hips and thighs, everything tensing and pulling in, waiting for that moment of explosion. I'm so wet.

Every sense is heightened as he finds brand new sensitive spots I never knew I had.

Barrett's eyes burn into mine as his tongue lands squarely on my clit, his middle finger stroking slightly inside me. I feel completely trapped by his thick arms, pinned by his huge body, so tiny and helpless, yet at the same time totally safe.

His eyes are tracking my every movement. He's paying attention to every noise I make. Every part of him is focused on my pleasure, and it's completely overwhelming. My heart hammers and my pulse pounds as I see Barrett realize how close I am.

Without stopping licking, he manages to growl, "Come for me, princess. *Now*."

I fall to pieces and my shriek echoes around the room as my thighs clamp around his ears. The force of my climax curls my shoulders forward, everything quivering right down to my toes as I stare into the eyes of the sexiest man I've ever known.

My man. The only person I've ever felt truly close to.

As the pulses of my incredible orgasm slowly recede, my smile feels almost wicked as I make a decision.

I'm not going to sleep until I make him feel this amazing as well.

12

BARRETT

As I kiss slowly along the curve of Sage's hip, tracing a meandering path back to her luscious lips, I can feel something different in the way she takes hold of my hair and shoulder. She clutches me closely, pulling my lips to hers with a new urgency that drives me wild.

Her legs wrap around me as I groan at the feeling of my throbbing cock nestled against her soft, wet pussy. Even through my boxer briefs, I can feel her heat. She wants me. The way she's writhing against me leaves no doubt whatsoever.

But we didn't even know each other a few days ago. I'm three times her size. She's only stuck with me because of an injured foot. I have to keep chanting these facts in the back of my mind to stop myself from giving in to temptation.

Another deep groan rumbles through me as her hand slithers down my chest. "What do you think you're doing, princess?"

"You told me that I could say stop at any time," she whispers with a saucy grin. "The same goes for you. Just say the word if you want me to go to sleep."

The tip of my shaft is peeking out the top of my briefs. She squirms, moving her curious hands down to push the fabric away. Then she grips my aching cock between both palms.

Sage's lovely blue eyes fly wide. "Wow," she breathes. "It feels...tight. Like it wants to explode."

"You have no idea." My back teeth are practically grinding as I try desperately to remain still.

Sage laughs, then pulls her tank top down to cover her stomach. She bats her eyelashes seductively as she looks up at me sweetly. "Why don't you pretend my hands are... something else? And you can come all over my stomach and I'll just throw this top in the bathtub after."

I wouldn't have thought it possible, but I become even more turned on by the fact that she thinks ahead like that.

Her thumb slides across the tip, rubbing in the pre-come that's gathering quickly. Then she tentatively strokes my length, arching her back to press her breasts against my body.

"If you don't want the real thing, you have to let me do something," she whispers saucily.

My one hand scoops under her lower back, the other behind her shoulders, clutching her sexy little body to me. I'm unable to hold back as our lips crush together, my tongue tangling with hers: my hips begin to rock of their own accord, thrusting into her hands.

Her sparkling eyes are wide with joy. I can't wait until they're lighting up from the feeling of me pumping into her snug little pussy.

Her soft hands feel incredible as she strokes me. I pump slowly, my balls already tightening as familiar sensations gather low in my core, but this is more intense. I've never had a hand job like this before. I cage her body with my arms, imagining that I'm rocking inside her.

She's *mine*. The fact rolls through me slowly with utter clarity, as if it's always been there. My girl. My precious woman that I'm going to care for forever.

I'm going to claim her, possess her, make her happy every day of her life...and always make her come so hard that her soft voice is hoarse from screaming my name in passion instead of screaming for help in the forest.

Reluctantly releasing her delicious lips, I pull back to stare into her eyes, feeling my shaft swelling beyond belief and my balls contract.

Sage winks. "Come for me, big guy," she demands sweetly.

My deep growl makes her eyes blaze. Her hands clench tighter as I fuck them harder, faster, then shake from head to toe as I come so hard I can feel it in the back of my calves.

"Princess," I groan, clutching her frantically as I grind and thrust as every single drop bursts from me.

I wonder if I've been too rough. Too crude. But Sage just looks delighted as she beams. "Wow! There was a lot more of it than I expected," she giggles.

I roll off her, and we both look down at the complete mess I've made of her tank top. How can she manage to look casually glamorous with her hair tangled everywhere, and my giant load splashed across her stomach?

"Sorry—" I begin, but she waves the apology away.

"Don't worry about it."

I help her peel off the shirt, then I toss it to soak in the bathtub. I also give myself a speedy rinse for good measure. I return with a warm washcloth, wiping gently across her hands, her stomach, then between her legs.

I slip into bed and arrange the blankets. Sage snuggles against me as if she never wants to leave. That works for me. She feels so perfect in every part of my life already.

I've never been one to get my hopes up. But I am now. I need her to stay with me and for this to work out.

For the first time ever, this surly, set-in-his-ways mountain man is ready for his life to change completely.

13

SAGE

Sitting in a beautiful house in the mountains while a gorgeous man makes me breakfast... Am I in a fairy-tale? Honestly, part of me wonders if I passed out in the forest and this is all a giant hallucination.

While we eat, Barrett tells me all about Old Hemlock Valley and its many features. He's not exactly subtle about it. Apparently Mrs. Fergus at the library will scour the Earth to order any books I want, and she'll be thrilled that I'm a fellow bird watcher.

There aren't a lot of clothing shops or camera stores, but Barrett has a big post office box for deliveries. He explains that there aren't a ton of restaurants and cafés around here, but the ones that are, are all excellent. He's clearly trying to sell me on the area. I don't know that he has to. Everything I've seen so far is wonderful.

My phone rings, and Barrett's slight smile turns to a scowl again when he glances at it. He jumps up to bring it to me, and I'm surprised to see that Carl is calling instead of his usual texting.

"Hello?"

"Sage. Where the fuck are you?"

Barrett takes our empty plates to the kitchen to give me a bit of privacy, but I know he's trying to listen in on our conversation.

"Kind of nearish Old Hemlock Valley," I say, not wanting to give him any specific location.

"I need you to meet me in Pinesley at noon. The gas station near Main and Sidney."

"Um..." I hesitate. "Then could you drive me back here?"

"Jesus fucking Christ," Carl snaps. "I just got finished setting you up with a ride back to Mackton. Don't they need you at the daycare?"

"Who would be willing to give me a ride to Mackton?"

"My friend Bill. He's making a delivery an hour north of there. He can drop you off."

Carl has become more and more invested with his "deliveries" lately, and it's honestly starting to creep me out. He's careful never to let any details slip, and I don't have the guts to ask. Well, I can stay in don't-ask-don't-tell mode for a little while longer.

On one hand, I know that I should at least go back to Mackton to pick up my things and make sure that Sheila has someone to cover for me at the daycare. But the thought of getting a ride with one of Carl's buddies is giving me a cold, sick feeling.

"No. I'm not driving all that way with a stranger."

I hear Barrett slip quietly from the kitchen to the bedroom, but he doesn't shut the door. Of course he's listening to my every word. I don't blame him.

"Dammit, Sage – I called in a favor to get you that ride."

I hate when he gets angry like this. It makes me feel like I'm seven years old and I've accidentally touched something that I didn't know was off limits.

"That wasn't our original plan. I was going to pick you up, then you and I were going to drive to Mackton together."

"Plans change. Deal with it. I don't care if you take the ride or not, as long as you get that goddamn car to Pinesley by noon." He sounds frantic. Desperate, even.

"Why does it have to be noon? Can't I have lunch first?"

"There are things that need to be sorted out by one o'clock today, and I need that car by noon. Don't you dare fuck this up for me, Sage. If you screw this deal for me, I will never speak to you again. Ever. Do you understand?"

"Yes," I whisper, just before he hangs up on me.

My phone hits the table with a clatter as tears fill my eyes. I already know my life is small and uninteresting, but still...my brother has a particular talent for making me feel utterly worthless.

Two gentle, heavy hands land on the back of my shoulders. "Let me help, Sage."

He massages me for a moment, then drops into the chair beside me. His eyes widen and his jaw clenches when he sees my expression. Reaching out slowly, his thumb glides under my eye to wipe away a tear. "Oh, baby, no. Please. Tell me what I can do."

"It's not your problem," I sniffle, trying to choke it all back. "I've been too much of a bother already. My family are nasty people, and they're not your concern."

He grips my hands, shaking them slightly. "Sage, *you* are my concern now. Understand that?"

"You barely know me. You have your whole life going on. Your own worries..."

My eyes fall closed and I try to compose myself, but Barrett shakes my fingers until I'm forced to look at him. "There are plenty of things that are hard for me to say. Maybe because I've never had cause to say them before. But now... Sage, I want you to be my concern. I want you in my life."

My chest feels tight. "How can you make a huge decision just like that? You've only known me for a few days."

He stares out the window for a moment. Then he turns back to me and smiles. "Here's the thing. I want to care for you. Protect you. I want you to be my girl." He's so sexy when he smiles with that intensity. "Do you want me to be your man?"

I'm already nodding. "Yes."

"You're just scared because this is all happening so fast?"

"Yes."

"Okay..." His hands are so warm and comforting as he gently strokes his thumb across my skin. "How about we assume that everything is going to work out? If you change your mind, you can tell me it's over, and I'll drive you back to Mackton, and we'll just stay friends."

Swallowing hard, I can't even speak, just nod fervently.

"Okay. Good. So given that we're operating under the assumption that I'm your man..." His expression tightens. "There's no way in *hell* any woman of mine is going to that godforsaken place on her own. And you're *not* driving all the way to Mackton with some scummy friend of your skeezy brother—"

He stops himself and frowns. "I'm sorry, princess. But if your brother is running deliveries around Pinesley like that, you know it isn't anything good."

I nod again. "That's exactly why I don't want you to meet Carl."

"Why not?"

My bottom lip quivers. "B-because I don't want you to think that I'm like him."

"Shhh, oh, baby, no." He slides our chairs closer to slip

an arm around me. "I'm not going to judge you for a second. But I have to keep you safe. I'm going to care for you until you tell me to stop. Okay?"

My awkward smile seems to relax him. "Okay."

"Good. Here's the plan. We'll take all your stuff out of your car. You'll drive there with me tailing you in the truck. I'll call you when we're close to give you directions. You drop off the car, and I bring you home."

"Sounds good." Crap. I still don't want him to meet Carl. With the badly done back alley tattoos all around his neck and the wild, frantic energy he usually has in his eyes, he just looks like trouble.

And for all of his rustic woodsman lifestyle, Barrett is quietly classy. Clean. Crisp.

His hand drops to my ankle. "Is your foot okay to drive?"

"Oh, sure. I won't put much weight on it at all."

"That's my girl."

Something warm and beautiful spills through me hearing those words. *His girl.* It makes me want to believe that everything is going to work out fine...so, so much.

I just have to figure out how to keep my brother away from...*my man.*

14

BARRETT

What usually would be a forty minute drive to Pinesley takes an hour, because I keep reminding Sage to drive slowly along the curvy mountain roads. Luckily, we left in plenty of time because I expected this to happen.

What I did *not* expect was the packages wrapped in black plastic that I found hidden in the trunk of the car when I cleared out the last of Sage's bags.

The bundles were badly hidden – some inside the spare tire, and a few more stuck up against the back corner. A large part of me wanted to take the car straight to the police to have it inspected. But if Carl is friends with dangerous people, I don't want to risk any of them being upset with Sage.

She's so open and trusting. I can see in her eyes that she still wants to have a relationship with her brother, since he's the only family she has left. But I could tell just from Sage's end of the conversation that he was being horrible to her... It was all I could do to not grab the phone and roar at him until his ears bled.

No. I'll remain calm, for Sage's sake. Once this is over, and she's completely moved in with me, I'll make sure she knows how a man should speak to a woman and how people are supposed to care for each other.

"Turn left onto Sidney Street," I say toward the phone sitting on the seat beside me. "The gas station will be ahead on the right."

"Okay. Thanks."

Sage is a cautious driver, which I appreciate. I've been attempting to be more chatty during the drive, which is a bit draining for me. I'm also a little concerned about her poor little foot.

"Everything all right, princess? You sound worried. Or are you just tired?"

Her car makes the left, then slows down even more. "Barrett, if I asked you to hang back and not meet my brother, would you be okay with that?"

This feels like an important moment. I keep asking Sage to tell me to stop if things are too much. I want her to feel like she has as much control over this relationship as I do. And I did already put my foot down about letting her come to this horrible place alone.

She sighs. "I can hear you making that grumbling noise right over the phone, you know."

"Sorry." Dammit, I'm going to have to do the right thing, no matter how wrong it feels. "How about this, princess – I'll just pull up on the other side of the parking lot and mind my own business here in the truck. But *you keep this call open.* Good enough?"

I can hear her sigh of relief. "Yes. Thank you."

Sage pulls into the gas station and heads toward the east side of the parking lot. There's an orange failed attempt at a muscle car parked there already with two scrawny guys leaning on the hood. I'm surprised the rust bucket can hold their weight.

I pull into the far side of the lot and park in a spot that gives me a clear view of them, and crank the volume on my phone.

"Cutting it pretty close, sis." The guy with the greasy hair and smudgy throat tattoos must be Carl. Charming.

"I'm ten minutes early." She sounds nervous. I hear rustling as she grabs her purse with her phone in it.

"Come on, come *on*," he hisses.

"Sorry," Sage says. "I have an injured foot." She swivels out of the seat to stand up slowly and carefully.

"Yo, is the dumb bitch gonna hurry up or what?" the guy in the cheap leather jacket snarls.

Instead of defending his sister, Carl cackles like a hyena. "Yeah, my little sis has always been slow. Clumsy, too. It's a wonder she was able to drive here without going off the road to chase after something shiny, or one of her stupid fucking birds."

The world turns red.

A slow blink.

Then I've never run so fast, crossing the parking lot in three heartbeats.

Another slow blink.

Two hard thumps as their heads bounce off the brick wall of the gas station. I'm holding them by the throats. I get a strong urge to close my hands on their windpipes.

Another slow blink.

And then a heavy hand lands with a solid thud on my shoulder.

"Breathe, Barrett. They're not worth it."

I whirl to see Jace Wolfe giving me a slow nod. "Whatever these two assholes did, I'm sure they deserve having their teeth knocked out for it. But it doesn't have to be by you. And it *really* doesn't have to be in front of this nice girl, who looks completely terrified."

Two slow blinks.

Finally a slithering thump. I set the jerks back on their feet, and turn toward Sage. Her beautiful eyes are huge, mouth open as she stares at me in disbelief.

Glancing back at Carl, I gave him a shove on the shoulder – just enough to remind him that I'm three times his size and could knock him into next week without breaking a sweat.

"If you're ever impolite to your sister again, you will have me to deal with."

"*And* all of his friends. I'm one of them," Jace growls, with a glare that could freeze the sun.

Leather Jacket Punk is already scrambling into his car and taking off.

Carl steps toward his car, but I stop him with one finger to the center of his chest. I turn to Sage. "Do you have everything you need?"

She nods, still speechless.

I remove my finger and grunt, "Stay away from Wolfe Mountain." He scrambles into the car and screeches out of the lot.

Slowly reaching for Sage, I notice that she lifts her hand to take mine, but doesn't stand as close to me as usual.

"What the hell are you doing here?" Jace asks. "I hate having to stop in Pinesley even for gas."

"Just clearing something up." I clap him on the shoulder. "Thanks. Almost lost it for a split second."

He nods. "I could tell. But it's never worth it." He turns to Sage and tips an imaginary cowboy hat. "Jace Wolfe at your service, ma'am."

"Um, Sage Campbell. Thank you." My poor baby sounds rattled.

Jace gives me a nod of farewell and heads back to the gas pumps as I turn to face Sage, gently holding her hands in mine. "Are you okay, princess?" I ask as softly as possible.

Her head nods gently.

"Were you frightened by how angry I got with Carl?"

Her head tips back and forth. "A little. But it was more that..." Her breath is shaky.

"Please tell me. I'm so sorry if I scared you, baby. I never want to do that. I don't think I've ever seen red like that before in my life."

"That's not it." Her voice is almost hollow. "I've just... never had anyone stand up for me before. Like...ever." Her lovely eyes fill with tears, causing a crushing sensation in the center of my chest.

Lifting her gently, I cradle her in my arms, cuddling her head against my shoulder. "Princess, I would go to the ends of the Earth for you. I'd defend you against an army."

"I know. I just still can't believe it."

"It's okay." I carry her back to the truck. Once we're seated side by side, I hold out my hand palm up, and am relieved at how quickly she takes it.

"Sage, I get the sense that you've been wandering. I don't wander. I'm planted like a tree. You could plant yourself in Old Hemlock Valley with me if you wanted. You wouldn't ever have to see Carl again."

She nods slowly, frowning. *Oh crap.* She doesn't like the idea of anything being final with the only family she has left. Maybe...

"Unless you want to check in with him every Christmas?" I ask gently. "Talk once a year, and we'll hope that he gets his act together?"

Her bottom lip trembles. "You'll hope with me?"

"Yes.."

Suddenly her lovely blue eyes are sparkling again. "You're pretty good at the compromise thing, did you know that?"

I half chuckle. "I did not. Guess I do now."

I hold out my arms, and she snuggles against me as I kiss the top of her hair. "Sage, I want you to be happy. And I hope that's with me."

She smiles up at me with that beam of sunshine in her eyes. "Pretty sure it will be."

15

―――――

SAGE

Boundaries. Lines. Barrett is very strict about staying on the trail, and now it makes sense.

On the drive back to his house, we decide that I'll block Carl's number for now, but reach out and text him at Christmas. That I'll never see him or speak to him without Barrett standing right beside me until we can tell that he's cleaned up his life. That if he continues down a path I don't like, I just won't speak to him again.

But we both hope he comes around. I love that Barrett isn't unilaterally anti-Carl. He just wants to be sure that I won't be hurt again. The thought of me being harmed seems to upset Barrett on such a deep level that I'm genuinely moved.

Barrett eventually tells me about the packages in my car. It makes me realize that if I hadn't drawn a line with Carl, I could have ended up in serious trouble. Barrett hasn't only rescued me from being hurt in the forest, but from the blinders I tend to wear when it comes to my brother.

We also chat about how between my shyness and Barrett's tendency to be quiet, communication is something we'll need to work on. We make a solemn vow to blurt things out even when it's awkward or stupid. We also agree that laughing with each other will get us through the weird bits.

Finally, we decide I'll call Sheila tomorrow, and figure out whether I should go back and work at the daycare for a few weeks until she finds a permanent replacement. We don't want her to be left in the lurch.

We.

We're a *we*.

We're making plans about *our* future!

By the time we get back to Barrett's house, my heart is singing like a yellow-throated warbler. Maybe even a rose-breasted Grosbeak – one of the few birds that sing even while nesting.

I love that he carries me inside and immediately checks the dressing on my foot. I love that he makes us a "pub grub" dinner of burgers and Caesar salad, while promising to take me out for a real date in just a few more days.

I love that I'm learning to read all the little details of his body language. The way his gaze flicks to me when he's trying to decide what to say. The way his jaw loosens a bit when he's trying to speak more softly. The way his eyes twinkle for a split second before he opens his mouth to laugh.

I love Barrett.

I appreciate how much he's willing to change for me. Not just little things like clearing out a drawer in the bedroom for me, or making a shopping list of my favorite foods. He's more talkative than he was the first few days. I feel that's huge for him.

Yet it feels much too soon to tell him how strongly I feel

about him. At least in words. As we get snuggled into bed, I realize there's another way to tell him.

His hand slips immediately under my silkiest tank top and slowly runs along my hip. "No underwear again." His dark voice is extra gritty. "Do I need to take you shopping?"

"I have plenty of underwear. Again, I just didn't see the point."

His fingers tighten around my outer thigh as he gives my leg a slight shake. "The thought of taking you shopping and you wearing clothes I bought for you turns me on."

Reaching out, I slowly skim my palm down his thickly muscled chest until it bumps into the top of his briefs. He's turned on, all right – his shaft is peeking out the top enough for me to rub my thumb across the tip.

"What do you think you're up to, princess?"

"Oh, about five foot four. You?"

That delicious grumble is so sexy when we're in bed. "A comedian, huh?" He kisses the tip of my nose while running his palm along my inner thigh. "Six foot four, actually." Something shifts in his eyes. "Which means I'm going to have to be very careful with you."

Turning, I place my other hand on his stubbled cheek. "I trust you completely, Barrett."

He nods, and I see another shift in his expressive eyes. His movements are agonizingly slow and deliberate as he pulls off my tank top, then slides off his shorts. When he lies beside me, I can feel the tension in his body. He wants me. Why is he still hesitating?

I moan softly as his hand slips between my legs, gently stroking just his fingertips through my folds.

"I don't have any condoms," he growls softly. "Haven't thought about something like this in years..."

"I'm on the pill," I whisper, feeling my cheeks turning

pink. "A few of the kids at the daycare were obviously accidents, and I got paranoid."

A wolfish grin lights up his eyes. "Good. I don't want a single thing between us, princess."

Even as his massive body moves over mine, caging me, I feel safe. Complete. My sensitive nipples scrape against Barrett's chest and my legs spread, telling him what I need.

Then he ducks down, spreading me wide as he devours my pussy. I grasp at his hair while he licks and kisses and sucks at my clit, my breath already getting ragged. The possessive way he scoops a hand under my thigh to pull my hip into position, he might as well tell me that I belong to him. Does he understand I feel the same way?

He's tasting me, exploring, as if he's trying to memorize my body. My chest squeezes from the look in his eyes as they lock with mine.

"Say it," I whisper. "Whatever you're holding back, say it."

The corners of his eyes crinkle slightly as he smiles. "*Mine.* That's what I'm thinking, princess. Mine. My pussy, my hot, gorgeous girl, my incredible ray of sunshine breaking through my cloudy moods."

Then he groans deeply, thrusting a finger inside me as he swirls his tongue around my clit, already knowing that it drives me wild.

He reaches up, knowing precisely when and how hard to pinch my nipples so the tiny bite of pain mixes with the pleasure, sending me into the stratosphere as I practically tear his hair out. The climax is so intense I almost panic, my body thrashing as he holds me down, licking steadily, until I finally grow still.

"Barrett..." I whisper as he crawls up my body, the thick trunk of his shaft landing on my hip bone. He shifts, pushing it down so that his length rubs against my oversensitive clit.

Something stops me from blurting out the thought that's been bouncing around my mind for hours...my surly, silent mountain man knows exactly what I need, even more than I do.

"Sage." The scrape of his rough voice makes me shiver with arousal. "You're already my girl. I want to be your man."

"Yes. That's exactly what I—"

"Love you." His eyes blaze as he hovers over me. "I love you so much already, princess. And months from now I'm going to love you even more."

I swallow hard before I answer. "I love you, too."

He smiles, then nods. "Then I guess that's all settled."

He reaches down to throw my leg around his hip, then drags the thick, blunt head of his cock through my wet pussy lips. I'm already twitching, gripping the back of his shoulders.

"I promise I will never hurt you, Sage. Just breathe."

Then he catches my lips against his, just before easing the head inside me. "So tight," he growls against my mouth. "So soft and wet and perfect. My sexy princess was made just for me."

I love the way he talks when we're in bed. I didn't know I needed it. I feel tiny and delicate with his hard body over mine, and try to relax enough to take his thickness. He's a huge beast of a man, but I'm so wet and eager for him that he sinks a few inches inside me, both of us moaning.

"Wow," I whisper, gripping his shoulders, encouraging him to keep going.

A deep shudder runs through Barrett and he pauses. Maybe he realizes the importance of this moment, and that

I'm so tight that he's really going to have to push to sink any deeper.

"I'm ready," I whisper. "Please... I want more."

He takes a moment to read my expression, then nods. "Okay. Hold onto me."

I carefully move my other leg around so that I can lock my ankles behind his firm ass. He scoops an arm under my shoulders, holding my body to his. Then I gasp, shaking as he crushes my lips with a ferocious kiss as he suddenly thrusts his hard, pulsing cock all the way into my untouched pussy.

For a moment, I can't breathe. Can't see. Fire flows through my veins, too many sensations flooding my nervous system at once.

Then I realize the base of his shaft is rubbing firmly against my clit. With the first stroke, I'm his. By the tenth, I'm moaning uncontrollably. By the twentieth, I'm already coming, wailing, falling apart, as Barrett's growling grumble fills me as much as his hard, massive cock.

The pressure is incredible, coming from all directions at once as I implode, shaking helplessly. It also feels like he's finally losing a bit of control, thrusting a little harder through my unbelievable climax.

In the haze of adrenaline and lust, a fragment of clarity appears in my mind. Listening to the way other people describe sex, it always sounded kind of dirty. But Barrett has only ever treated me like a treasure. Like I'm precious and important to him.

From the first moment we met, he really has treated me like a princess.

Now I want to treat him like a king.

16

BARRETT

Somehow I manage to keep my movements steady and relatively gentle as Sage squirms and wriggles wildly while coming all over my cock.

It's the most incredible feeling on the planet, but I can't release into her yet. Can't let her think that I'm some guy that comes fast and won't give his lady everything she needs. Still, it's so hard to not drive into her that my hips almost ache from the effort of holding back.

Her back arches as a last jerking shiver goes through her, and I hold still inside her, my shaft as deep as it will go.

"Is that what you needed, princess?" Pulling my length almost all the way out, then gliding inside again, she's still unbelievably tight. "Your snug little pussy feels incredible around my cock."

"Yeah?" she breathes, blinking up at me. "Good. Because I feel that you need a bit more."

She squeezes me with her inner muscles, and I inhale sharply. "Dammit, princess. I'm trying to be gentle here."

She grins at me saucily. "What if I don't want you to be gentle?" She digs a fingernail slightly into my shoulder, tracing a line down my back. "What if we were out in the forest together, and you got so horny you had to shove me up against a tree and take me then and there?"

Godammit...

In a second, I've scooped her up, still plunged deep inside her as I carry her a few steps from the bed to the wall. With her back pressed against a wooden beam, I lift her higher. I use my entire lower body to thrust freely, every stroke making her luscious tits bounce.

"Like this?"

Sage gasps, gripping me as she locks her ankles around me, moving with me. "*Yeah*. Just like this. Take me any way you want."

My loud growl makes her eyes blaze. "I will. Any way, any time I want." Her pussy flutters around me. Damn, she likes that. "When we go for hikes, I'll pack a blanket so that I can take you right there on the forest floor."

"Uh-huh..." she moans. She's so beautiful, all flushed and wild as she opens herself to me.

"And I'll take you up against a tree just like this. Your hot little squeals will scare away the birds."

Leaning in, I bring my lips to her ear. "If there's hikers around, you're going to have to be so quiet, princess. Can you do that for me? Come on my cock over and over again while not making a sound?"

She whimpers, squirming between the hardwood and my hard wood. "Maybe."

The tight velvety grip of her pussy is driving me to the edge hard and fast. Not even her softness, her sweetness, can take the savage edge off my deep, possessive thrusts. This moment of bonding is so clear and pure, like a fierce summer storm driving everything else away.

Her mouth hangs open, eyes glassy as she twists her

hips. I slide my hand between us. "Is this what you need, sexy? Just a bit of pressure right...*here*?"

My middle finger fluttering against her clit is all it takes to trigger another climax. "Yes," she shrieks. "Barrett... please...oh...yes!!!"

It's impossible to hold back any longer. Once she stops shaking, her snug wet pussy still quivering like crazy around me, I hold her hips steady. Driving deep and hard, my sexy, sweet girl smiles at me, nodding and panting. "More. I want it all. Please."

Fuck me.

Hearing such a sweet girl beg for my cock with that sexy look in her eyes is too much. My balls have been so tense for so long, but finally they unlock. Thrusting deep into her tight heaven, I watch her bouncing breasts for a few wonderful moments before ravaging her mouth.

My entire body shudders as I spurt hot bursts of my seed deep inside her. "Mine," I roar, overcome with pleasure as I plunge deep. "My perfect princess."

Sage's eyes grow wide as she gasps brokenly, her lips swollen from our kissing. My hips can't stop pumping and she comes again, squeezing me as if she's milking my shaft.

Kissing along her throat as she cries out my name, I feel a wave pass through me that's even bigger than the climax of a lifetime crashing over me.

We are together. Completely. Forever. Sure, we're going to get married and have kids and all that great, amazing stuff. But in this perfect moment, I can feel that Sage's decision is already made.

"I love you," I murmur gently against her lips as we grow still.

Her voice is barely a whisper. "I love you too, Barrett."

Then her eyes snap all the way open. "But I think I need

to go to the bathroom for a second or I'm going to leak all over the place." I start to chuckle, and she smacks my shoulder. "Seriously, dude. If I laugh, your floor is toast."

I carry her to the bathroom door before setting her down. She's trying not to giggle as she shuts the door between us.

After a few minutes, she returns and crawls into bed with me. I love how after all of that frantic intensity, Sage curls up my arms and grows still and quiet.

"If you do go back to Mackton to work at your friend's daycare for a while, I'll go with you," I murmur, stroking her back gently. "We can stay in a hotel. Check out all of the local restaurants."

Her delicate face lights up. "Really?"

"Why not? I'm a homebody, but I do like checking out the world sometimes, too." My fingers trail slowly around her hip. "Especially different restaurants. Baz was going on again about the incredible food at this winter chalet he visits every year. Got me thinking I should get out a bit more."

Sage grins, her bright eyes sparkling. "So it's not just me dragging you out of your shell, it's for the sake of amazing food as well? Good. That makes me feel a lot better."

"Baby, I don't mind changing for you." Rocking her gently, her soft, naked body feels so perfect against mine. "I was long overdue for a change, to be honest. People are supposed to grow and evolve, not stay as still as a stone."

"Yeah..." Her fingers walk across my chest. "Wouldn't want moss growing all over you."

"I know you won't ever let that happen, princess." Taking her delicate fingers, I kiss across her left hand. "Hey – isn't there something called a princess cut diamond? That almost rings half a bell."

She shakes her head quickly. "Yes, but no. You can't possibly be thinking about fancy rings and stuff."

"Sure I can."

Her sexy bottom lip wobbles. "Barrett," she whispers, "I don't have any money. I'm not in debt or anything, but other than my clothes, and a few boxes of knick knacks, the only thing I had in the world that was worth anything was my share of that crappy old car."

Her breath is shaky. "Meanwhile, you've got a house and land and a truck and who knows what else. I don't have anything to bring to this relationship. So I can't accept any—"

I cut her off with a soft, breathy kiss. "Shh, baby. You've got so much that you'll bring. For a start, you'll help me help the community by bringing in the right kind of tourists." I smile at her. "You're going to help with promotion, and signage that people will actually want to read. Help us protect the trails, while still letting hikers enjoy them safely. Most importantly, you're going to help me be less grouchy when I have to deal with...what do you call them again?"

Her eyebrow raises. "People?"

"People. Yeah. That's it. We're going to make a great team."

My lips brush across her forehead as she laughs. "I still don't think that's exactly equal. My photos, blogging, and sign creating powers versus your house and land."

"You're a wonderful chef's assistant. Honestly, you're the best spinach shredder I've ever worked with. You can't put a price on that."

She smacks my chest lightly. "As soon as you let me walk again, I'm definitely going to be pulling my weight with housework."

"As soon as your foot is healed, our first priority is for me to take you down to the wilderness store to get you some proper hiking boots. Then we're going to go through and clear all of the trails together."

I'm already addicted to her soft sweet giggle. "Yes! You can hack back the high branches and I'll stay low to pick up any litter."

"Don't forget to leave some of your three stick markers whenever there's a bend in the trail and people need to be directed."

"Sure." Her head rests against my shoulder, and after a moment she sighs. "It's funny,you know."

"What is, baby?"

"Just a week ago, I hadn't even met you. I figured I'd be at the daycare for at least another year and then...who knows? I just sort of followed Carl wherever he went, or where friends could help me find a job, and a place to live, or whatever. I wandered around pretty aimlessly. But now I'm actively choosing to be somewhere." She grins. "It feels really good."

"I'm glad." My arm squeezes her gently. "Because *you* feel really good. Like you belong here."

"I honestly think I do."

Sage's hand strokes my chest for a while, then slowly stops as her eyes drift closed. Her breath becomes slower, deeper, as she gently sinks into sleep. I listen for a while to her soft sounds, to the forest outside, to the wind rushing over the mountain.

Rescuing a fairy princess from an evil wizard, even if it was her brother? *Check.*

Getting the most beautiful woman I've ever seen to fall in love with me, and stay here with me? *Check.*

Being lucky enough to find a woman who understands

my cloudy moods, my surly attitude, and my grumbles? *Check.*

I hold back my chuckle, not wanting to wake her.

Am I going to look up what a princess cut diamond looks like, and start shopping for an engagement ring as soon as I can?

Check and double check.

EPILOGUE
SAGE

"What do we do if we see a snail or a frog?" Our four-year-old grins up at me, tugging at the bottom of his little jean jacket. "Tell you, but don't touch it."

I grin. "Perfect. And do we drop anything on the trail?"

"Nope." He's heard this one a million times already and shakes his head vigorously. "Never mess up the woods."

"That's right, sport." Barrett scoops up the miniature version of himself to reach for the outline of a hand on the sign. "Ready?"

Noah high fives the sign, his sweet rosy-cheeked face beaming. "I'll be good."

We've all spent a lot of time in the forest from day one and he's bouncing with excitement to be going out on the trails with us on his own two feet today, not in a sling or piggybacked by Daddy. "All growed up," as he put it.

His father and I got married in one of the little wild-flower-strewn fields, with a small party back at the house afterward. By then I'd met over half the town, all of whom were pleasantly surprised that Barrett was getting married and settling down.

Even though he's always had a reputation as a loner, it's obvious that they respect him. All of Old Hemlock Valley knows that they can call Barrett for help any time of day or night and he'll be there immediately to fix any situation.

Nearly everyone I've met on this section of the mountain is ready to help each other out at a moment's notice. It feels incredible to have a circle of people who genuinely care for their neighbors, and the town.

The first Christmas Barrett and I were together, I called Carl on Christmas Eve. He didn't answer. The next year his number had been disconnected. The following year, Barrett somehow got some of his acquaintances to track him down, so that I knew he was all right.

It turns out that several of his friends got busted for a certain delivery, but Carl was late for it, so he wasn't there at the time. He was very lucky there.

He took it as a sign that he needed a fresh start and moved to New Mexico to work in a restaurant belonging to an old high school friend. These days, the only deliveries that he's concerned about are fresh vegetables.

My brother is now exactly how I want him: happy, healthy, and thousands of miles away from us. Our Christmas Eve video calls are just the right amount of contact...at least, for now. Someday, after he's been stable and responsible for several years, Barrett and I will decide together when it's right for him to meet our family properly.

Noah's little feet pad gently over the leaves and twigs in his miniature hiking boots as we walk slowly, staring in awe at a squirrel, a chipmunk, and a goldfinch. We've reminded him repeatedly to be quiet in the forest, so his sudden squeal of delight is thankfully at half the usual volume. "Mommy, look – the bird has a triangle!"

We all pause, watching as the blue-winged warbler flits from branch to branch. Barrett crouches down to murmur, "That's probably the great-great-great grandson of the bird Mommy was chasing on the day we met."

Noah's eyes are huge as he waves. "Hi there, birdie!"

Instead of flying away, the warbler looks at him with interest, hopping one branch closer to stare.

Slowly raising my camera, we all stay still as I quickly snap several shots. Then I cautiously back up and to the side, getting a shot of Noah pointing out the bird to Barrett, with the triangle-shouldered warbler in the frame too.

It's the best photo of my entire life.

Then I feel a kick from a tiny foot deep in my belly, and correct myself.

It's the best *so far*. But maybe an even better one is yet to come.

You'll meet Barrett's brother Baz in the *Wolfe Mountain Chalet series.*
You'll meet Riggs again in *Possessed by the Surly Pilot*, and Jace in *Found by the Surly Ranger*.

POSSESSED BY THE SURLY PILOT

We lurch to the left, my body falling into his. He wraps his arms around me, holding me close as he caresses my back. Since we're in the bulkhead row at the front of the plane, nobody can see us. It feels like we're totally alone.

"I'm so sorry—"

His strong hand slips up the back of my neck, sending all sorts of inappropriate and ill-timed sensations swirling through me as his fingers tangle in my hair. "Don't be. I'll take care of you."

I don't know which is worse, for Riggs to think I'm trembling because I'm terrified, or because I've never been held by such a sexy man before. Though really, both are true. So does it matter?

He pulls away just enough to look into my eyes. Maybe the poor guy was hoping for a quiet flight and now he's stuck with me. "Would leaning up against me help, Olivia?"

I'm already nodding. "Yeah. You're, um, warm."

He looks over his shoulder, but the flight attendants have disappeared, probably strapped in themselves. One strong hand massages my knee, and the other caresses my back, making me feel enveloped by this huge man.

"Do you always fly first class?"

I stifle a snort. "Please. This is my first flight ever. The check in lady saw how nervous I was and upgraded me so I'd have more room."

"Here." He moves the armrest up and out of the way so that I can slide closer to him.

"Thanks." It's like I'm in another world – normally I would never just cuddle up with a stranger. Yet as the plane lurches again, it feels natural to take comfort in the arms of a strong man who really does seem to think everything is fine.

"Big breath in, then blow it out slowly."

Mmm... Why do I love that commanding tone so much? Something about it makes me tingle in deep places that I've never paid any attention to. I've been told what to do and controlled my entire life, but Riggs is very different from my father's overbearing suffocation. So again, I obey without thinking.

I dip my head to exhale into the broad chest of this total stranger who is caressing me as if he already knows me. As if he's dreamed about touching me for years.

"I shouldn't be doing this," he murmurs, reading my mind. "I should stop."

"Please don't." I look up to meet his midnight eyes. "There's *something*..." I trail off, lost for words. He's a mountain man. I can almost smell the forest around him.

"I feel it too." His eyes tighten. "But I shouldn't be taking advantage."

He tries to pull away, but I yank him closer. "Please. The way you're touching me... It's taking me away from all this."

Possessed by the Surly Pilot is available now.

Don't miss:
Found by the Surly Ranger
Saved by the Surly Medic *(Aug. 7th, 2024)*

Available for pre-order - Coming this Fall / Winter:
Protected by the Surly Carpenter
Sheltered by the Surly Forester

ALSO BY HALEY TRAVIS

Book links at haleytravisromance.com

Saved by the Surly Medic

Jonah Wolfe is sexy, smart... and clearly not the chatty type. He's grouchy with others, but utterly sweet with me. Every touch, every caress whether innocent or not, makes my pulse surge. He wants me. Yet his overprotectiveness is totally over the top considering we barely know each other.

Thin Ice - Winter Heat at Wolfe Mountain Chalet

He's a total stranger. Until I slip and fall into his arms, and then into his bed.

He claims he's a loner, yet from the second he growls, "You're mine," into my ear, I want it to be true.

The Lumberjack's Quirky Girl

I probably shouldn't have ogled Braden Oakley's big axe. *Oops.*

Tall as a redwood and built like a moose, the devastatingly gorgeous lumberjack should have nothing in common with little miss artsy-pants—aka, *me.* So how come the harder I try to stay away, the more I end up wrapped up in his muscled arms begging for more of his hard...wood?

Meet all four HOT Oakley brothers HERE.

Possessing My Lily

From the second her delicate body thumped into my chest, I knew Lily was mine.

Her New Bodyguard: Jackson

It was supposed to be a simple personal security job. But Ashley

was so sexy and innocent that my need to care for her was far
more than professional.

Mackton Mechanics

Rev your engines and get ready to fall for these hot mechanics!
These huge, rough men are comfortable working with steel. What
will happen when they're tinkering with a sweet girl's heart
instead of a motor?

Fake Summer Wife

I'd always been too timid. But when a gorgeous man needed a
favor and asked me out in front of the whole diner, I had to say
yes... I would be his phony wife for one night.

For new release updates from Amazon, go to the author's page,
then click **+Follow** near the top left.

Please join the mailing list at haleytravisromance.com for new
releases, updates, discounts & freebies!

www.ingramcontent.com/pod-product-compliance
Lightning Source LLC
Chambersburg PA
CBHW021021160726
47994CB00006B/2606